DEATH OF A COWBOY

RON CANNON

TATE PUBLISHING, LLC

FOREWORD

Several years ago, while on vacation, this story began to develop in my mind. By the end of the week I had most of the story in mind. Out of the blue, without any intension of even writing anything, I begin to put the words in my computer. It wasn't until then I knew God had put this story on my mind.

Based on my grandparents and something grandmother told my grandfather, the story is set decades before either one of them were born. I found the year 1876 to be a more interesting time in which the cowboy seems more colorful. Although the names within the book are close to real names, all the characters in the book are fictional along with the story itself. The only thing I know, and you should know, is my grandparents were devoted to God and each other until their death.

PREFACE

The Silver Spur Ranch was a large Texas ranch, covering forty square miles of rolling hills. Mesquite trees, sagebrush, and cactus covered most of the ranch, which made working cattle difficult.

There was a large ranch home with a barn, corral, and bunkhouse for the cowboys. The ranch house had a long porch that extended the full length in front of the house with four bedrooms upstairs. Each bedroom had a big poster bed, a wardrobe, and a washbasin on a stand with a mirror. Downstairs was a great-room with a large rock fireplace, and off to one side was a large dining area with a long table that could seat twelve to fifteen people. Behind the dining area to the back of the house was the kitchen. The kitchen had three worktables, shelves for pots and pans, a wood stove for cooking meals, and a small table with four chairs used when someone wanted to eat or have coffee. The door at the back of the house led to a privy.

The barn had a loft, several stalls and a tack

room. The corral beside the barn housed the horses that were used daily. Next to the corral was a somewhat round pen with a post in the center where the green horses were broke. There was usually a half dozen a year to break.

Lost Creek was a small town just a short distance to the northeast of the ranch. Lost Creek had a livery, bank, hotel, a general mercantile, and a saloon along with a few houses and couple of other places of business. At the end of the street, there was a small white church and a schoolhouse next to it. They usually handled the necessities there in town, but if there were something special needed, they would order it in on a freight wagon. Lost Creek didn't have a railroad yet, so the cattle were driven north into Kansas where there was a railhead to market the cattle.

CHAPTER ONE

We had just finished spring roundup and the smell of branding the cattle filled the air. That stench of burning hair was a smell I never had gotten used to, but I did like the aroma of mesquite wood burning in the fire used to heat the branding irons.

We were all preparing for the long cattle drive. Over three hundred miles to Dodge City, and at ten to twelve miles a day, it would take us a month or more to get the herd there for the train east.

I galloped up to the chuck wagon on a large brown gelding with a white forehead and socks, pulling the reigns back hard to stop. He kicked up dirt that drifted almost to the wagon. I climbed out of my Texas saddle and tied up to a wheel.

"Cookie, we should go into town for supplies. We'll be leaving early in the morning."

"I'll get my horses and be right with you, Wil."

Cookie's real name was Hank Kroft. He was getting on up in years but it was hard to tell. His face was brown and weathered looking. His hair and mustache were graying, and he was tall and slender. He made some meals like cow tail stew, sourdough biscuits, and red bean pie. I would like to have said it was good, but sometimes it was just barely edible. He did cook plenty, and when you had worked hard all day, you got hungry and ate anything that was in front of you.

"Ok, Wil. I'm ready to go."

I climbed back in the saddle of my horse, Dobbs.

"Heya, getup."

The ride into Lost Creek was about an hour one way with not much to see. There were just hills with sagebrush, cactus, and some mesquite trees. Most of the mesquites are in the lows along dry runoff creek beds. We saw a jackrabbit and a coyote off in the distance. Some buzzards were flying around above something that had died or had been killed. An occasional dust devil reminded us of some of the storms that we had in the past.

"Wil, do ya think the spring storms are about done for now?"

"Yeah, Cookie. I think we'll be okay this trip. I have seen bad storms this late in spring only a few times. Even then it was just strong winds and heavy rains. We didn't have that ice stuff falling from the sky."

"Yep, I remember back when we had some of that ice falling and all sorts of things going on. I was sure glad that I had that wagon to get under. Y'all didn't have anything but your horse and saddle to keep you from getting beat up by all that ice that fell that time."

"Yeah, Cookie. I still ended up black and blue all over. I felt sorry for Dobbs because the only thing I could do for him was get him under the edge of a mesquite tree. If I had not had my hat, I would have had some knots on my head."

"Wil, that ice had to be as big around as a dollar."

"Cookie, some of it was that big; most was somewhat smaller."

"I knew when that wall of dirt started our way out of the southwest we were going to be in fer some kind of storm."

"Yeah, Cookie. That was some storm. A wild kind of electricity sure spooked the herd. It took us miles to get the herd turned and stopped after that stampede. We worked well into the next morning rounding up strays."

"We lost quite a few head of cattle that time, didn't we?"

"Near a hundred, Cookie. It's the largest amount that I have ever lost to a stampede. I think there were a couple of the boys hurt, but not very bad."

There was a silence for a long while as we continued to town.

"Say, Wil, have you ever thought about getting married and having a place of your own?"

"I thought about it with the girl I had seen a few times. She up and died and I never had a chance to even talk to her about it. After that I haven't called on any women that I thought would be the one. I suppose I will see the one I think would be right for me some day. But until that day comes, I am happy with the way things are."

"You think it will be love at first sight for you, Wil, when you see the right one?"

I drew out my revolver and shot a rattlesnake that I had seen just in front of us. The gunshot spooked the horses a bit. There were a lot of snakes out there, and you really had to watch so your horse didn't get snake bit and throw you off. Most of the time, the snakes heard you coming and they would go away from you. We must have come upon this one asleep in the shade.

"Good shoot'n, Wil. I didn't see that one."

"How about you, Cookie? You ever think of getting married?"

"I don't think I'm the marrying kind, but you never know. I might meet just the right one someday and just up and do it. I don't mind dancing with them at the saloon and at the ranch parties, but I haven't seen one that suits me."

When we went over a hill, the town was in a little valley below. It didn't look like there were many people in town. The street wasn't very busy at all. A few cowboys and a farmer or two was all that I saw on the street.

"Well, Cookie, I'm going to the blacksmith down to the livery and get a shoe replaced on Dobbs' right front foot while you're in the Dry Goods Mercantile. I'll meet you back here."

The owner of the Dry Goods Mercantile was Sam. He was a short, balding man that was broad and somewhat heavy.

"Howdy, Sam. I need to get a few things before we head north. Give me two sacks of flour, sugar, beans, coffee, chewing tobacco, and some grain. Oh, give me some salt, too. I think that will do for this time. Just put that on the ranch account," Cookie said.

"Ok, Hank. I'll have that for you right away. Y'all plan on leaving out first light?"

"Knowing Wil, it will be long before that. He likes to get an early start when we head out on the drive."

"Howdy, Wil."

"Howdy, Sam."

"Who was the young lady that just left out of here? I don't think I have seen her around before."

"Oh, that's Bradley's daughter, Wil. She doesn't get into town much. Not sure what her name is. They have a farm a few miles out."

"She is a fine looking lady, Sam. Maybe I'll run into her before we leave town. Let me have some cartridges for my rifle. I don't expect trouble, but you never know."

"Yeah, Wil. The Apache are still coming out of the New Mexico Territory to raid into Texas. Well boys, that's got everything on your list. I'll help you out with it."

"Sam, I sure appreciate it. We'll see you when we get back. Cookie, I'm going to get my horse and we will be on our way."

"Ok, Wil. I'm going to the saloon to have a quick one before we leave out."

Spurs jingled as I walked down the wooden

boardwalk to the livery. When I was approaching the front of the bank, that fine lady was on her way out. I thought about introducing myself to her.

"Howdy, ma'am." I reached up as to salute and touched the brim of my hat. "I'm Wil Gannon. I don't think we have met."

"No, I'm Claudia Bradley. We have a farm just west of town."

"I work for the Silver Spur Ranch. We are going to leave in the morning on a drive to Dodge City. Do you suppose that I could call on you when we return?"

"Oh, I don't think so, Mr. Gannon. Being a cowboy is not an honorable profession. Farming is an honorable profession."

"Good day, ma'am. I hope to see you when I return."

"Good day, Mr. Gannon."

A man walked up from behind her who might have been her father.

"Who was that man you were talking to, Claudia?"

"Oh, just some handsome cowboy, father."

CHAPTER TWO

I walked across the sod street to the large barn like structure with a hitching post and water trough out front. A corral was on the left side. Above the door of the livery was a loft. It had a covered area to the right that was a makeshift blacksmith shop.

"Cletus, is my horse ready yet?"

Cletus was a large man with large muscles in his arms from the blacksmith work. The cowhide apron he wore kept him from burning up his clothes. Even though the temperature was still on the cool side, he was sweating from the work he was doing.

"Yep, Wil. He's ready to go."

"What do I owe you, Cletus?"

"A dollar and two bits. I gave him some grain and a quick curry."

"Thanks, Cletus. I'll see you when we return from Dodge."

"Have a good trip."

I rode up the street wondering what she meant

by "not an honorable profession." I was an honorable man doing an honest days work. I just didn't get it. I just couldn't stop thinking about it.

"Sorry I took so long, Cookie. I didn't mean to leave you waiting."

"I just now got here Wil. I was afraid that I was going to be keeping you."

"Ok, let's move out, Cookie. It will be dark before long and I want to check on things at the ranch before I ride back out to the herd. Talking about those storms reminded me that I should get the rest of my rain gear."

"Yeah Wil, there are some things I need from the ranch that I had forgotten to load the other day."

We ambled our way towards the ranch and talked about first one thing, then another.

"Wil, have you ever had to kill someone? I don't mean just for doing, but because you had a good reason."

"Cookie, that is a subject I really don't like to talk about. But to answer your question, no. I try to live by the Code of the West, meaning, if someone has done something wrong, I will do what I can to bring justice since there's not any law or lawmen out here. The only law or lawmen we have out here are the Texas Rangers. I think they concentrate to the south and west of here. They are stretched a little thin since they have been fending off Comanche and Kiowa. Maybe we won't have to encounter any of them along the way."

I really didn't know how we got on the subject of killing someone, but we did. Just the idea of having to kill someone didn't set well with me. I didn't know why I was that way. Just was.

Coming up on the ranch, the sun was getting low in the western sky. I saw a horse tied up in front of the house. It looked like a golden palomino like the one my good friend, Jacob Norton, rode. Jake was a drover for most of the big ranches around. He was a tall man with dark brown hair. He wore a Montana most the time. You could see his brown hair on his collar. His face was brown from the sun, and he had wrinkles around his eyes caused from squinting at the sun. A scar on the left side of his chin was the result of a fight some years back.

I rode up to the house and tied up as Cookie went on to the bunkhouse to gather the things he needed. As I stepped up onto the porch, Jake and the ranch owner, John Elder, came out the door.

"Afternoon, John. Howdy, Jake. John, I didn't know you had gotten Jake to head up this drive."

"Yep, I thought it would be a lot easier for you if you had his help. He knows the trail really well and is between things right now."

"That's a good idea, John. It is a lot of work for one person to run a drive. Not that I mind being trail boss and running the outfit, but it is nice to have help. You know how good friends we are. Jake will be good company."

"Yeah, Wil. It'll give us a chance to catch up. It's been a couple of years since I have been over this way. I don't remember you having that mustache the last time."

"It's left over after one winter when I grew a face full of hair and decided not to shave the mustache."

"Well, you boys best get out to the camp with the herd so y'all can line things out fore morning."

"Yeah, John. Cookie is getting last minute things and we'll be on our way. Ready Jake?"

"Yep, Wil. Got your back."

We mounted our horses and started for the bunkhouse as Cookie was loading the last few things on the packhorse.

"Cookie, you remember Jacob Norton, drover for most outfits around?"

"Yeah, Wil. I think I remember him over here a few years back. How you doing, Jake?"

"Good, Cookie. You still fix those beans?"

"Yep, sure do. And if you're lucky, you might get a biscuit to go with um."

I was glad that John had hired Jake to help with the drive. I didn't know what it was, but I had a weird feeling about the drive. Something just didn't feel right. I knew we didn't have much sleep with working long days getting ready, but I didn't think it was the lack of sleep. I had a lot on my mind, and now I guessed I'd have a few more things to think about. I just couldn't get what Claudia said off my mind and Cookie asking me about killing someone. I hoped it was just my being tired. I would have liked the trip to go smoothly. With all my thinking, I hadn't heard a word of the conversation that Cookie and Jake had been having.

"Wil, did you hear what we said?"

"Oh, I'm, sorry boys. I just was in deep thought here. What did you say?"

"We were just talking about how many cattle and horses we have to drive this time. I was just telling Jake I wasn't really sure about the count, so we were asking you, Wil."

"We have about fifty horses in our Remuda. We have about twenty-five hundred or so cattle. The herd is not as big as we had hoped for, but we hear the price for cattle are up this year, so we should make a good amount. I am sure the men will get their wage and maybe a bonus if we get there and the price is still up. They will all be glad to get into Dodge. It is so much bigger than Lost Creek. They seem to find more to do there."

CHAPTER THREE

"Cookie, I guess you better rustle up something for our supper. I bet the boys are pretty hungry about now."

"I'll have it ready in just a little while, Wil. I'm sure they will all be in about the time it's ready."

"Jake and I are going to look the herd over to see how things are going. We'll let some of the boys that are watching the herd come in. They can split up the watch for tonight, and we will eat when someone comes back out."

We were watching the herd just wandering around. I saw Jake just a little way over from me. I heard one of the other hands off to the distance singing a tune that sounded familiar but I couldn't think of the name of the song. All at once I saw a rider coming toward me from the direction of the camp. He was coming at a pretty fast pace.

When he got to me, he pulled up the reigns

and stopped just short of me. Slim had come out from camp.

Slim had come by that name honestly. He was a tall, slender man with a dark mustache. I would think he was in his thirties, and he had been working cattle most of his life.

"Howdy, Slim. What's all the hurry?"

"Wil, there's a couple of Texas Rangers at the camp. They asked to speak to the one in charge, so Cookie sent me out to get you."

"Thanks, Slim. I'm going over to get Jake and we'll see what they want. You stay here and help with watch."

I kicked my horse into a gallop and headed over to where I had seen Jake. I pulled up with a cloud of dust and stopped next to Jake.

"Jake, let's go. There are a couple of Texas Rangers at camp asking to talk to us."

The skies were almost dark, but you could just see well enough to make the outlines of everything. A little ways over you could see the light of the fire that Cookie had going. When we came up to the camp, the rangers were squatting next to the fire drinking a cup of coffee. Cookie was always polite that way, offering strangers coffee and sometimes a meal. We rode up to the wagon, tied up our horses, and walked over to where the rangers were. They both had the Texas Ranger star in the circle on their badge. They both had revolvers they wore low on their hip. They weren't large men, but I would say they were about my size, medium height, and medium build.

"Howdy, boys. I'm Wil Gannon and this is our drover, Jacob Norton. What can we do for you?"

"I'm Marty Slone and this is Sandy Packman. We are here because there is a complaint about some missing cattle at a ranch not far from here. A large burly man that rides a black stallion, and a half Indian man on a paint head up a gang that took about a hundred head of their cattle. When we were in Lost Creek they said that y'all were heading out in the morning for Dodge, we thought we should come talk to you guys and check your herd to make sure there were not any of the missing cattle here before y'all leave out. Y'all don't mind leaving out a day later, do you?"

"No, not at all, boys. We will cooperate in any way we can to help you boys figure this thing out. I can personally tell you that you won't find any of their cattle here, unless they were brought in while I was in town earlier today."

"Just the same, Wil. We'll check your herd in the morning."

"Marty, that is fine with us. Y'all stay, have supper, and bed down here with us if you like. We can ride out when it gets light and check for any stock that is not a part of our herd."

"Thanks, Wil. We appreciate your hospitality. I think we will take you up on that."

We got a plate of beans and a biscuit. We sat down near the fire, ate, and visited a while. That time of the year was pretty cool after the sun went down, so that fire felt pretty good. A few of the boys were playing some cards, and one was playing a guitar. In the distance we heard coyotes yelping, cattle calling low, and the whinny of a horse on occasion. With very little moon, it was really dark past where the fire gave off light. It didn't take me long to fall asleep. The next thing I knew, it was just about daylight. I heard Cookie getting around over at the chuck wagon. He just about had breakfast ready. I smelled coffee and biscuits cooking. I got up and ambled my way over to where the coffee was.

"Cookie, is the coffee ready yet?"

"Yes, Wil. I'll get you a cup."

"Thanks, Cookie. I suppose the others will be up soon."

"Yep. The smell of breakfast always gets them up."

He had some bacon cooked and was cooking some eggs. Some of the others had gotten up. I turned and looked. Jake was headed this way.

"Morning, Jake. Did you sleep well?"

He must have had some pain in his neck or something the way he was rubbing it.

"Yep. I slept ok, I guess. I got a kink in my neck though. I must have slept crooked."

"Jake, you'll have it worked out in no time. When we get to moving the cattle, you will have the soreness worked out."

"I was sure hoping to be on the way today, Wil, but I don't want them to think we stole any cattle from your neighbors. I heard talk about those guys some time back. They were talking about stolen cattle. They killed some guys and stole their horses too."

"Jake, I hope we don't run into them on the drive. I have enough to worry about without them."

"Worrying about the Indians, terrain, and weather is enough to have on your mind, Wil."

"Morning, Marty. You and Sandy ready to get this done?"

"Morning, boys. Bout as ready as ever, I guess."

"Sandy, you and Marty get a plate and let's eat breakfast. Then we'll go out so y'all can look things over."

"Thanks, Wil. Don't mind if we do. I am hungry this morning."

"Get all you want. Cookie always fixes plenty."

"I'm not very hungry, but I do think I'll have some just the same."

When we all had finished breakfast, I told the men what was going on and what we were going to do. Some of them grumbled a little, but they were all ready to get it done so we could be on our way the next morning. They got on their horses and went to round the cattle up close so they could look them over. Twenty-five hundred head or so would take a while to look at. Since we were not going to be able to leave till morning, I was sure we could get done well before dark.

"Ok, Wil. Sandy and I are ready to do this. I'll get on one side and Sandy on the other, and your boys can push them though between us. That way we will be able to check them out from both sides."

"Sounds good, Marty. The boys will have them up this way about the time we get mounted up and ready."

We all went over to where we had the horses tied to a line and saddled them up. I got mounted up first and headed over where the boys were with the cattle and told them to start them moving our way. I turned and headed back toward the rangers and Jake. I decided to get on one side, with Marty and Jake on the other with Sandy. The cattle moved through slowly as we watched. We were at it about two thirds of the day and we didn't see anything that looked like anyone else's cattle. We only had a few more and would be done. I thought they were satisfied after about the first thousand head or so, but had to continue to be sure for themselves and the neighbor. Just as the last few came by, Marty and Sandy turned and came over to me.

"Wil, I guess that about does it for us here. I suppose we will have to look somewhere else. I think we will go by your neighbor's place and then into town. Maybe we can pick up something at their ranch that will give us a clue as to where to look. If not, maybe someone in town has heard something that will help us. Either way, y'all have a good trip up to Dodge City."

"Thanks, Marty. I am sorry we can't be of any more help to y'all. Maybe there will be something or someone that can help y'all. Good luck and I hope y'all can catch those boys. I don't think we want to have to deal with them on the trail. Ok, some of you boys stay with the herd. The rest can go eat and get some rest. You can trade off in a while. How bout you, Jake? Think you are ready to eat?"

"Yep. I think my stomach feels like it is an empty pit. I could eat most anything."

"That's good to hear, Jake, because it could be almost anything that Cookie has fixed. It could even be fried rattlesnake."

When we arrived at camp, some of the boys had already gotten a plate and were eating. It had been a long while since breakfast and I was pretty hungry. I kept thinking about those boys that had stolen those cattle. They couldn't sell them around here, and it was closer to drive them to Kansas than it was to Mexico. I just hoped they didn't try to steal some of our herd. They probably had branded over on the stolen cattle so no one could tell.

"Howdy, Cookie. I'm ready for supper. Working through dinner, I built up a big appetite."

"Here go, Wil. I'll have some coffee in just a minute."

"Thanks, Cookie. Looks good. Steak, beans, and a biscuit should just hit the spot."

"Here's some coffee, Wil."

"Thanks. Jake, get a plate and sit down. It's time we rest for a while."

"I don't mind if I do. I'm about give out."

"Jake, I've been thinking about those boys that stole those cattle. I think since it's so far for them to go to Mexico they might go to Kansas after they stop to brand over the cattle. They may even try to get some more cattle along the way. I think we should keep a close watch just in case."

"I think you're right, Wil. It's likely that they might add to what they have along the way."

We finished our meal and visited while we drank

some coffee. Most of the boys had come in, with the exception of the few that were out on watch. I waited until most were finished with their meal before I decided to tell them about what we were thinking.

"Well boys, as you know, the Rangers were here looking for stolen cattle. We didn't have any in our herd of course, but they didn't know that. Jake and I feel that these thieves might be taking the cattle to Kansas. We also think that they may add some to what they stole along their way. They will be branding over to get by. We will have to be on the look out for these boys and make sure they don't steal any of our herd. You boys on night watch be very careful and know where each other are at all times. We don't want to mistake someone for the thieves. We will be leaving out before first light, so check your gear and get some rest. Slim, you get four more boys and relieve those on watch now. I'll have someone relieve you about midnight."

"Ok, Wil."

I laid there thinking about everything: the rustlers, the weather, the rangers, and the lady I had met in town. I guess that was about the time I fell asleep. I woke up and looked at my watch. It was about a quarter of twelve.

"Wake up, time for watch."

"Ok, Wil.

"That time already, Wil?"

"Yep, it's that time."

"Tom, wake up, time for watch. Wake up, Cody and Dan. Take watch until breakfast."

"Ok, Wil."

The moon was about half full. It gave off a little more light than it did the night before. I was lying back on my gear, looking at the night sky. I suppose it wasn't long before I went back to sleep. The next thing I knew, someone was giving me a nudge.

"Wil, wake up. It's not long before daylight. Breakfast is ready."

"Ok, Cookie. I'll be right there."

I got up and was ready to eat. It sure smelled good. By the time I got to the chuck wagon, Cookie had a plate ready.

"Thanks, Cookie. Sure looks good."

I sat down with my breakfast. Jake had gotten up and he was on his way over to join me.

"Morning, Jake. Sleep well?"

"Yep, pretty good I guess. I doubt I get that good of sleep from here until we get to Dodge."

"Yeah, I know what you mean. We'll be lucky to get a couple of hours sleep per night. Some of you boys go relieve the boys on watch for breakfast."

"Ok, Wil. Come on boys. Let's go."

We had finished breakfast just about the time the boys on watch came in. I decided to saddle Dobbs and get ready to move out. I had given him some feed last evening when we came in. I decided to give him some oats and a little hay while I saddled him up. I picked up a bucket of water on my way over, then got him some feed. Dobbs started to eat when I picked up the blanket and put it on his back, followed by the saddle.

"Easy boy. I'm just putting the saddle on."

He moved his head up and down as if he were

approving, then went back to eating. I saddled him and headed over to get my bedroll and other gear. When I returned, he had finished eating. He looked around as I put my gear on the saddle. I climbed in the saddle, spun him around, and headed out toward the herd. I wanted to look things over. I turned and looked; Jake was riding over my way.

"Well, Jake, with the possibility of Indians, thieves, and bad weather, are you ready to start this herd north?"

"Yeah, Wil. Might as well. I think we are as ready as we can get. We've dealt with bad weather and Indians, so I know what to expect. I've not dealt with thieves before. I guess we'll handle it best we can if it comes up. I'm going out ahead. I'll see you sometime around noon."

"Ok, Jake. We'll point this herd north and be right behind you. Slim, Cody, Tom, Dan, pass the word. Let's move 'um out."

CHAPTER FOUR

We whistled and shouted and the cattle began to move slowly. We remained on the outskirts of the herd to keep them going in the direction that we wanted. I stayed in front on one side as we began north. Jake was well in front of the herd, so he could choose the way. By my calculations, we would be on the Red River in about six days, maybe seven. We had some good spring rains, so the river might be up. The grass was good, and there were a few water holes that still had plenty of water. The sun should be up in another hour, but there was plenty of light. I dropped back and checked on how it was going. I looked around for strays and things that might have caused some problem. I guess it was hard not to think about things that could have been a problem. The sun was about up now. I could see off at a distance there were some heavy clouds and some rain falling. It looked like it was moving away from us. I heard the bawling of a calf somewhere nearby. I turned and went to the sound that I heard. Sure enough, in a gully there was a calf that had gotten separated from its mother. I climbed down from Dobbs and stepped down in the gully to help it out. I lifted it up and gave it a nudge. It didn't take it long to find its mother. I climbed back in the saddle, and I was thinking how long I was going to have to spend in it on the drive. As I got older, it was harder to spend all day in the saddle. It made it easy to think about doing something else. Maybe farming wasn't such a bad idea. What was I thinking about? I had done this all my life one way or another. It was crazy how that lady in Lost Creek had got me thinking that way. I worked my way to the back of the herd. Back there the dust was pretty heavy. I covered my nose and mouth with my bandana to keep from inhaling all the dust. Slim and Cody were there in the back pushing the cattle. I gave them a nod and moved on to the other side and began to work my way back toward the front. The sun had gotten high in the sky. The way my belly felt, it must have been close to noon. Cookie had moved ahead of the herd and had probably gotten lunch ready.

"Tom, y'all hold the herd up at that watering hole just over there. We'll take lunch and rest for a little while."

"Ok, Wil. That sounds good."

I saw Cookie on the little hilltop. When I was riding over to the wagon, I saw Jake headed back from his scouting. I climbed down and tied Dobbs to the wagon.

"Here ya go, Wil."

"Thanks, Cookie."

I went over and sat down with my lunch.

"Howdy, Jake. How's it looking for us up there?"

"It looks to be okay in the direction we are headed. There's a good spot to bed them down just a few miles out. We should be there just about dark."

"Did you see any sign of Indians ahead?"

"No, Wil. But I did see some tracks like someone had come through here not long ago with a small herd."

"Jake, are you thinking what I am thinking?"

"Yeah. I bet it is those thieves."

"We'll continue to have extra men on watch at night just in case."

I finished and rested for just a little while. Jake had decided to go back out after just a few minutes of rest. He never had been able to sit around long. Most of the men had finished and headed back to the herd. I got back on Dobbs and headed toward the herd as they started moving north again. I fell in to help keep them all together. We had been trailing the herd a while since lunch when I saw Tom coming toward me.

"What's up, Tom?"

"It's Dan. He's hurt. He fell off his horse and hit his head. I think he hurt his arm, too. There must have been a snake that startled his horse or something."

"Find Cookie and have him see to Dan. He can ride in the wagon for now."

"Ok, Wil."

Well, we hadn't even gotten through one day and problems had come up. What's next? Things could have been worse. Indians could have attacked us. Thank

God we hadn't seen any so far. The sun was getting low, and we were getting close to that spot Jake talked about bedding them down. Jake joined us just a little ways back and he was leading the way. I moved over toward Jake about the time we were moving them to a watering hole for the night.

"We had a man hurt today, Jake. Dan fell off his horse and hurt his head, possibly an arm too. He's on the wagon with Cookie."

"Do you think he is hurt very bad, Wil?"

"I don't know yet. I haven't talked to Cookie."

"While we have them bedding the herd down, let's go to the wagon and see how he is."

"Ok, Jake. I'm with you."

We rode over to the wagon. I saw Dan lying over to one side and Cookie was still fixing supper. The way Dan was moving, I supposed he was not hurt very badly.

"Howdy, Dan. How are you feeling?"

"Ok, Wil. I just have a big knot on my head and sprang my arm. I don't think anything is broken."

"That's good, Dan. I am glad you are doing okay. Maybe you will be able to be back to the herd in a few days."

"I think so. I just hope Cookie can put up with me that long."

"Oh, if Cookie gets tired of you, he'll just throw you off the wagon."

"Really?"

"Ha, ha! No, I don't think he is apt to do that. He is probably glad to have some company."

"Yeah, Wil. It's good to have someone to talk to besides the horses and the wind. Well, supper is ready, so come and get it."

"I am ready, Cookie. I have worked up a big appetite."

"Me too, Jake."

We got a plate and sat down to eat and rest. All we did was ride and eat. Keeping the herd together and the strays pushed up was hard work.

"Wil, I've seen some more signs of that small herd still heading north."

"I know it must be those thieves."

"Well, most likely it is because most herds headed for market are larger than their herd. Ranchers wouldn't push a small herd that far."

"You're right, Jake. Most ranchers keep their cattle close to their own place."

"We may run into them in a few days at the pace they are keeping. They stopped a few times. It looked like they left the herd with a couple of boys and then returned. They didn't bring any more cattle with them when they came back, so I'm guessing they're scouting around for some more cattle. I didn't see any tracks headed this way, but that doesn't mean they didn't. I could have missed some tracks if they swung around wide."

"That's possible, Jake. Not much telling what this bunch is going to do. Stealing cattle in the middle of the night is one thing. But coming in guns blazing, killing someone, then stealing cattle is another."

"Yeah, Wil. If they were going to steal some

cattle, they should come in and take them at night. No sense in anyone getting hurt over cattle. Although, if we were to see them coming in, that doesn't mean that we won't try to stop them."

"Living by the Code of the West, we're bound to do something if we were to see them."

We were finally at the Red River after a long six days. I was glad that we didn't have any real trouble getting there. That thing with Dan getting thrown from his horse wasn't such a bad deal to happen. I meant, things could have been worse. Dan was doing fine and went back to work. The rains and the spring thaw in the mountains had the Red River up quite a bit.

"Wil, we can bring the cattle up a little ways to the wide spot where the river gets shallow. We should be able to cross there without much trouble. I don't think there is any quicksand in that area."

"Yeah, Jake. I agree. That seems to be the best way."

"I am still seeing those boys' tracks with the cattle every now and again. They are still headed north and are not far ahead of us. I didn't see where they crossed the river, but there are tracks on the other side out a ways from the river."

"Well, I think once we get the herd across the river we should bed them down here and move on in the morning."

"That sounds good to me, Wil. I am ready for a little rest. It's been a long day."

Jake and I went over to the herd to help guide them to the crossing place. We slowly drove the cattle across the river until they were all across. Just a little way over, I saw Cookie had set up the chuck wagon and was fixing our meal for the evening. When we got them all settled and ready for the night, I headed for camp. Jake had already made his way over there. I tied Dobbs to the line, unsaddled him, and gave him a curry. Then I went for a plate.

"Wil, I've seen some tracks that look like Indians had come into this area about ten miles or so from here. Maybe they will be clear of the area when we get there."

"I sure hope so, Jake. I don't like having to fight the Indians unless there is no way out. Did it look as though there were very many of them?"

"I think there were probably ten or twelve of them. It's just a small party. They may have seen the tracks of the boys that we suspect stole the cattle and decided to trail them to see what they could get."

"That suits me, Jake. Maybe it will keep them off our back. By the way, what do you think we are eating tonight?"

"Wil, I think he fixed rattle snake to go with these beans."

"It's not bad. I have had some things worse than this. I think it sounds worse than it taste."

"Yeah, not bad. It's really pretty good."

"I think I'm going to get some sleep now and help with watch later so it will give some of the boys a little break."

I lie there looking up at the stars, thinking about a little of everything. The last thing on my mind before I dozed off, were the Indians. I woke about midnight and put my saddle on Dobbs so I could go on watch. The moon had been full but was getting smaller. It was still light enough that you could see fairly well. I saw Slim and Tom just a little ways over. One of the other boys was down from them, but I could not see well enough to tell who it was. Over the other way in a distance, there were a few more boys but I could barely see them. I heard them singing a little tune to the cattle. I thought if the Indians or thieves came, at least we would be able to see them coming. Of course, they could have seen us also. We wandered in and out of the cattle, keeping them calm and watching. It was almost daylight and the night had gone without any trouble, thank God. I headed in for breakfast as some of the other boys were coming out to relieve us.

"Morning, Jake. Did you sleep well?"

"Yeah, Wil. I guess I did. I think I could have used a few more hours rest, but I can catch up when we get to Dodge City."

"I hear that. I know it is a long way to go, but I can't wait until it's over. I guess I'm always ready for it to get over with when we are on a drive."

"We better get started, Wil. It'll be daylight soon."

"Yeah, we need to get moving."

"Okay, boys. Lets get these cattle on the move."

CHAPTER FIVE

We had been in the Oklahoma Territory for a few days, and it had been run of the mill. I would rather expect trouble and not have it than not to expect trouble and have it. We came up to a place that looked like there had been some trouble. Jake rode over my way and stopped.

"Wil, I think we need to find out what happened here to see if they need any help."

"Ok, Jake. Let's go."

When we were riding up to the house, I could see there were only two of them. It looked like a man and a woman. I didn't see anyone else.

"Howdy, folks. I'm Jake Norton and this is Wil Gannon. We are taking a herd north to Dodge City. Our herd is just a little ways over there. Looks like you might have had some trouble here."

"Yes, we had some Indians come through here. By the way, my name is Nate Woodman and this is my wife, Christine. We hid out when we saw them coming.

If we hadn't hid out they probably would have killed us. They just stole our livestock and burned the barn. I think they got a few things from the house. I am glad that they didn't see us. We are expecting a child in the fall."

"You folks are very lucky. If they had seen you, they would have killed you both and taken your scalps."

"I didn't think about what all they would have done, Mr. Gannon. I just knew we couldn't defend ourselves from that many."

"How many do you think there were?"

"I counted at least ten. Could have been more, Mr. Norton."

"Have you seen any other herds coming through here headed north, Mr. Woodman?"

"We did see a small herd in the distance about three or four days ago headed north. Why do you ask, Mr. Norton?"

"We think those are the boys that stole some cattle back in Texas and headed for Kansas with them to sell. They have been ahead of us the whole time. We expect they may try to steal some more cattle before they get to Kansas."

"Do y'all need anything before we go?"

"No, Mr. Norton. I think we'll be ok. Thanks for asking."

"When we get back to the herd, I'm going to send someone back with a couple of horses. I do think you need them out here since the Indians stole yours. That is the least we can do for you folks."

"Thank you very much, Mr. Gannon. I don't know how we'll ever repay you."

"Don't worry about it. You can feed us a meal next time we're by here."

"We can do that."

"Wil, we better get back to the herd. We have a ways to go before dark."

"Yeah, Jake. We need to go and be on the lookout for Indians for sure. Mr. Woodman, you and your wife take care."

"Sure thing, Mr. Gannon. Y'all have a safe journey."

I couldn't help thinking on the way back to the herd that it must be hard for a couple way out here with nothing or no one around for miles. It was a nice little farm. I wouldn't mind having a little place like that back in Texas. When Jake and I fell back in with the herd, we sent a couple of the boys back with some horses. We trailed cattle until almost dark and headed in.

"That was a bad deal for that couple back there, but do you really think that we should have left some of our stock? That will cut into our profit, Wil."

"Yeah, Jake. I do think that they need the horses. It's just my nature to take care of folks that are in bad shape. If I have to make up the money out of my wages, then so be it. They were sure lucky to get away with their lives. The Indians don't often miss seeing someone. I sure hope they make it. They were a nice couple. I would hate to know that they were killed by the Indians."

"Ok, Wil. I'll ride out in the morning and see what's ahead. We don't want any surprises."

"Jake, we need to know where the Indians are and if those cattle thieves are near."

"Wil, I'm going on watch now to relieve some of the boys. You get some rest and I'll see you in the morning."

"Ok, Jake. See you in the morning."

When I lie down to get some rest, I could not forget that couple we came across. They were just trying to make a life for themselves out there, and the Indians were trying to take it from them. They were saved by a power greater than that of man, that was for sure. Jake could locate some tracks and find out where the Indians were. He could locate those we thought were the cattle thieves, too. Knowing where they were would give us some peace of mind. I must have dozed off because the next thing I had on my mind was food cooking. I woke up and got some coffee.

"Wil, Jake has already gone scouting. He said to keep the herd pointing north and he would see you by supper time."

"Thanks, Cookie. I'll have some breakfast, then get things rolling for the day."

"Ok, Wil."

I finished breakfast and saddled Dobbs. The cattle sounded a little restless and the morning air seemed different. I couldn't put my finger on it, but something seemed strange. I mounted up and saw that most of the men were ready to push on.

"Ok boys. Move 'em out."

The herd began to move with the whistling and yelling. The sun was not fully up yet, but you could see some orange in the east. The birds were making some noise as they began to feed. Some of the trees were still in bloom and the wildflowers were coming out. We trailed the cattle all day stopping only to eat lunch. Jake rode up about dark and removed his saddle for the night. He came over for a plate and sat down beside me.

"You look tired, Jake."

"I am after today's ride. I picked up the trail of those Indians that had raided the Woodman's place. It looked as though they were headed west. Maybe they were going back to their camp in Texas or New Mexico. We can always hope so. I also picked up the trail of those boys pushing that other herd. I rode up close enough to see that there were about five of them. The men the Rangers described were there."

"I wish that had not been the case, Jake. We may end up having to bring them to justice or hang them ourselves. I had really hoped that job would not fall on us. About how far are they ahead of us?"

"They are about a day's ride out. It looks like they have been camped there for a couple of days. They may know we're back here and are trying to let us get closer so they can steal some of our herd, Wil."

"We'll be ready for them if they try anything, Jake. I think we need to move on as if there was nothing wrong."

"That's probably a good idea, Wil. If we make some changes they may think we are on to them. I'll ride back out tomorrow and keep a watch on them so we know where they are."

"Well, I'm going on watch and come in at midnight. If I don't see you in the morning, be careful. These boys might kill you if they see you."

"Ok, Wil. See you tomorrow."

When I rode out for watch, I thought about how the drive was already harder than some I had been on in the past. I hadn't expected to have to worry about thieves as well as Indians. I worried too much. I guess that was part of being in charge. I just didn't want to lose any of them. I guess that feeling I had that morning wasn't anything. I turned in about midnight and woke up to a light rain. From the looks of it, we were going to have rain most of the day.

"Morning, Cookie. It looks like it's going to be a wet day."

"Yeah, Wil. I think you're right. Driving cattle is hard enough without having rain, too."

"Well, we'll get through it. We have in the past."

"Guess you're right."

"Thanks for the breakfast, Cookie. Better get going."

"Ok, Wil. See you later."

CHAPTER SIX

We began to move out, but it was really slow with the rain and the mud. Some of the runoff creeks were full and would make it difficult. We pushed cattle most of the day in the rain. It was some time after mid-afternoon when it stopped. I knew we hadn't moved far, maybe six or eight miles. The rain had made it miserable for all of us. Even with the rain gear I was soaked to the bone and cold. That time of the year, the rain was still cool. By suppertime I was ready to get by the fire to dry out some and warm up. Even though the rain had stopped, it remained cloudy so it didn't warm up much, if any. We pushed the cattle until it was dark, then bedded them in a little valley. I headed over to where I had seen Cookie set up. Jake had come in and was near the fire. I got some coffee and joined him.

"Miserable day, don't you think?"

"Yeah, Wil. A gray and weary day."

"Were you able to track those boys with the other herd?"

"No, the rain washed out any real tracks there might have been. I don't have any idea where they are now. They could be behind us, or way up north somewhere. They may try to use the rain to their advantage."

"That's not good, Jake. I think we need a few more boys on watch tonight just in case. Why don't you watch until midnight with the boys and wake me then, and I'll watch with them until breakfast."

"That's ok with me. Let's eat."

After we had eaten, I stretched out and fell asleep. It seemed as though I had just laid down good and Jake was shaking me.

"It's midnight, Wil. Everything's quiet but there's no moon, so it's very dark out there."

"Ok, Jake. Get some rest."

I left Dobbs saddled up just in case I had to take off in a hurry. Just as I was about to ride off I heard a couple of shots. That would make the cattle a little jumpy if it didn't get them into a stampede. I had hoped that wouldn't happen. With the mud, it would be very difficult to control them.

"Did you hear that, Jake?"

"Yep, I'm right behind you."

We rode in the direction of the shots to find the cattle jumpy, but they weren't trying to stampede. Slim and some others were coming back.

"What happened, Slim?"

Slim was out of breath.

"I seen someone trying to ease some of the cattle out of the herd and when I went in their direction, they fired a couple of shots and took off with the cattle. We gave chase, but we lost them in the darkness."

"Are you ok?"

"I think so, Wil. One of the bullets grazed Tom."

"How 'bout it, Tom. You ok?"

"It just grazed my shoulder, Wil. I'll be ok."

"Go let Cookie put something on it."

"Wil, we'll have to wait until we get some light to track 'um. Maybe they won't get far."

"Yeah, it's too dark to see anything now."

I guess we were lucky that the herd didn't stampede when the guns were fired. After that, everyone was up and out watching the herd. Cookie had even gotten around and made coffee and was getting things ready to make breakfast. I don't think anyone could have slept anyway. We rode for a few hours keeping watch, but nothing else happened. It was about sun up, so we headed in to eat and got some ammunition for our rifles.

"Jake, you ready to head out?"

"Yep, let's go, Wil. Maybe we can find those boys."

We followed their tracks for about ten miles or so but lost them not long after that. I didn't know how they could just disappear that easily. We trailed back to where we had last seen tracks and looked. They just disappeared as though they had fallen in a hole and it closed up.

"What do you think, Wil?"

"I don't know. I don't understand how they can disappear like that."

"I think we need to get back to the herd, Wil. They may be coming back for some more."

"They could be, but I don't think they would so soon after last night, Jake."

"That might be just what they want us to think, Wil."

"Don't know, could be."

It was late in the day and the sun was low. The herd was coming up on a good watering hole, so we eased them over there for the night. Jake and I remained vigilant until way after dark. I worked my way over to where Jake was.

"Well Jake, I don't know if they are coming back or not."

"If they do, it will probably be late, Wil."

"I think we need to go to camp, then come back out just before midnight, Jake."

"Yeah, that would be good. I am starving, Wil."

After we had eaten, we stretched out and rested for a little while before going back to watch. We remained awake the rest of the night. In the morning, Jake headed back out to scout. We continued for days without another sign of the cattle thieves or Indians in the middle of the Oklahoma Territory. By mid-afternoon, we saw clouds building off in the distance. I didn't think a lot about it until I saw a roll of dirt coming our way. I turned and yelled.

"Keep the herd in tight. We are in for a big blow."

46

I no sooner got it out when it hit. The herd began to get restless. The clouds built up and then the rain hit. Light rain at first, then heavy. We were able to keep the herd somewhat calm, but they seemed really jumpy. Small pellets of ice began to fall from the sky, and the herd began to move around in a circle. The rain got really light and the wind seemed to get almost calm. Then I saw it. A big funnel cloud came across about ten or twelve miles out from us. The herd broke from the circle and began to head in the opposite direction of the funnel. We began to run with them to keep them together as best we could. We ran for miles before the storm had finally passed. It took us a little while to get the herd calm and stopped. About dark we decided to stop for the night. Cookie had to be back where we were before we started running with the herd. I guess it will be biscuits and water, or whatever else we might have in our saddlebags for supper tonight.

"Ok, boys, cold supper tonight. Eat whatever you have in your saddle bags."

Jake was still out scouting when the storm hit. I just hoped he didn't get caught in the twister. The storm hit so fast that we didn't have time to put on our rain gear. I was soaked and had gotten cold. I gathered some wood and started a fire to warm up and dry out. When I began to gather wood, some of the other boys began to bring in some wood also. In just a little while we had a nice fire going. One of the boys said he had a coffeepot and some coffee to warm us inside, and the fire to dry us on the outside. The boys split up the watch and I stretched out in front of the fire. It didn't take long for me to dry out some and get warm. I guess I fell asleep because the next thing I knew, one of the boys was shaking me and telling me it was time for my watch. I got up and headed out. It was a dark night because there was no moon. I could barely see some of the other boys across the way. They were probably as tired as I was. I guess the cattle were even tired. They seemed to be really quiet tonight. After what seemed like a long night, I rode over and woke the other boys. The sun was about to come up. We got started back in the direction we had been going before the storm. About a half a day we were back where we were before the storm hit. Just ahead, Cookie had lunch ready, and I figured everyone was ready for something hot. We finished lunch and got back to the drive. Late that afternoon, Jake rode up.

"Howdy, Jake. I was worried that you might have gotten caught up in that twister that we had seen."

"No, but I was pretty close when it hit. Not long after I ran into a couple, Russ O'Bannon and his wife, Christal. They had their house and barn blown away. They had seen it coming so they got in their root cellar. They only have a few chickens and what they had in the root cellar. Everything else was blown away."

"I think we need to see if we can help them out. How long until we are near their place?"

"I think we should be at their place about noon, Wil."

We had supper, took our watch, and slept. The sun was really bright the next morning. We had breakfast and got on the way. It seemed like it was getting really hot and muggy. All of us were wet from sweat. The dust from the drive was sticking to us. It was forming mud. There was a watering hole just ahead, so that was a good place to stop for a rest.

I was washing the mud from my face when Jake came up.

"Howdy Jake."

"Looks like you got pretty dirty today, Wil."

"Yeah, sweat and dirt make you muddy."

"Those folks that I told you about last evening just live over there about a mile." He pointed in the direction of their place. I guessed that to be northeast of where we were.

"Jake, I think we should eat lunch, round up some stock, then go over with a meal for them. You know how I am about helping out people."

Dan and Tom rounded up the stock and we headed for the O'Bannon place. They looked to be gathering up what they could of their things that had been blown around by the storm. Most of the corral was still there, so we drove the stock in. We began to fix what was down so their stock didn't get away. While we were fixing the corral, they came over.

"What's going on here, Jake?"

"Mr. O'Bannon, we brought you some stock from our herd and a couple of horses to help get you by. Cookie sent over some lunch for you, also."

"Christal, look what they have brought us. Isn't that nice of them?"

"Oh, they shouldn't have. That's too much."

"Mr. and Mrs. O'Bannon, this is my good friend,

Wil Gannon. Wil, this is Russ O'Bannon and his wife, Christal."

Mr. O'Bannon was a large man. He was muscular and had light, reddish-brown hair. His wife, Mrs. O'Bannon was somewhat smaller than myself with blond hair. I could tell she had been a city girl most of her life by the way she had not been aged by the wilderness. They looked to be a nice couple.

"Good to meet you sir, ma'am," I said as I touched the brim of my hat and nodded. "Is there anything we can help y'all with before we move on?"

"If you don't mind, we could use some help getting the wagon rolled over. I don't think there is anything else that we need. We'll use the root cellar for shelter until we get the house rebuilt."

"We could help y'all with your house if you needed us."

"No, Jake. I think what y'all have done for us is more than enough."

"Ok, boys. Let's get that wagon back up."

"Thanks very much for your help. Here is something for y'all from our root cellar. I hope you like molasses and pickled eggs."

"That sounds really good, ma'am. I haven't had any of that for a while. The molasses will go well with the biscuits that Cookie makes, and I'm sure that all of us will enjoy the pickled eggs."

"Y'all stop by if you're ever in these parts again."

"We'll do just that, Mr. O'Bannon."

"Ready to get back to the herd, Wil?"

"Yep, we best get going. We'll be seeing you folks. Take care."

"I guess that couple gets their supplies from Woods Station."

"Yeah, it's not far from here."

"We should be able to get to the Washita River by dark, Wil."

"Yeah, we'll be able to get there easily by dark, Jake."

CHAPTER SEVEN

On the way back to the herd, I couldn't help thinking how lucky that couple had been. I was just glad we were able to help them out.

We trailed the cattle until almost dark when we saw a man riding in from the west. It seemed that he was by himself, nobody else around. When he approached us, neither Jake nor I recognized him. He reached in for something from his pockets. About that time, Jake drew his gun.

"Hold it right there, partner."

"Wait, don't shoot. I'm just going for my cigarette rolling."

"Oh, sorry fella.'"

"Jake is a bit jumpy about strangers just now. What can we do for you?"

He crossed one leg over the saddle horn and began to roll a cigarette. I was amazed at how he seemed to roll it almost one handed. Once he had it rolled, which took no time at all, he put it to mouth and lit it.

"I came from Texas and seen you boys here. Thought I might get some work. I've worked ranches and drives. I'd make a good hand."

"What do you think, Jake? Can we use another hand?"

"Yeah, I suppose we could use another hand considering all that could happen."

"You're hired, cowboy. What's your name?"

"Chris Toddle, sir."

"Chris, I'm Wil Gannon. Most people call me Wil. This is Jacob Norton. We call him Jake."

"You can get with Slim and he will line you out on where he wants you."

"Ok, Wil."

"Slim is the man right over there on the large white stallion."

When Chris was riding over to Slim, I wondered what a young man was doing way out there. That seemed an unlikely place to meet a stranger. With the chance that we might have run into Indians or those rustlers, we could have used all the help we could get. We had to worry about crossing the river. The Washita River was very high.

"Jake, did you find us a place to cross the Washita River?"

"Yep, we should be able to cross just east of here. It looks to be shallow over there."

"I guess we'll find out in the morning."

"I can sure smell that coffee, Wil. You ready for some?"

"Yeah, I could use a cup."

We rode over to camp for coffee and a meal. I took the early watch with the boys. I rode watch without any problems. I woke Jake a little after midnight. It had been about an hour when I heard a few gunshots. I jumped to my feet and saddled Dobbs. The cattle were spooked a little from the shots. By the time I got out to where I heard the shots, Jake and some of the boys were coming in from the west.

"What happened, Jake?"

"Indians stole some of our horses. I shot one of them. We gave chase but they lost us. Not enough light to see. We'll pick up their trail in the morning when we can see."

We rode over where he had shot one of the Indians the night before and found that they were Apache. He was dead. We quickly found the trail and followed it for hours, which led to a small canyon where we found them holed up waiting for some others. We decided to rush them and take the horses back. There were six of them and only five of us, but we had the element of surprise on our side.

"You ready, Jake?"

"'Bout as ready as I'll ever be."

"I figured we could run straight at 'em, guns blazing, then run with the horses."

"Wil, is that the best plan you can come up with? We could get shot."

"We are apt to get shot no matter what. I just figured if they weren't expecting us we might have a good chance."

"Maybe so, but I still don't like it."

We ran at them as fast and hard as we could, guns blazing. We shot two of them right off. Dead or not, we left out with the horses. We ended up with their horses and ours in the mix. One of the boys was wounded in the shoulder, but he was ok. If they were waiting on some others, I hoped they didn't decide to come back at us. We caught up with the herd a few hours later. They had crossed the river and were moving slowly north. I had the wounded man, Al Marley go to the chuck wagon for Cookie to tend to him. Al was a nice guy and really quiet most of the time. He was the kind of man that would do anything for you. I turned to Jake.

"Al is the only one that got hurt. We were really lucky that more of us weren't shot or even killed."

"Yeah, Wil. If we had not caught them off guard there might have been more of us hurt. I guess your idea was a good one after all."

"I do come up with a good plan every now and then."

"Wil, we have a long way to go and I hope you have a plan every time we have something come up."

"Jake, you could come up with the next one. I don't want to steal all the glory."

"Glory? Is that what we are calling it? Kind of sounds like bragging."

"No, no. I didn't mean it like that Jake. Oh, I best just shut up before I get in any deeper."

"Ha, ha, ha."

Jake had his laugh, but I knew he was just joking around with me. He was that way sometimes. I really didn't mean that to sound like I was bragging. I hoped that we didn't need a plan for anything else. You never knew what was ahead of you. We had a pretty good day with sun and very little wind. Sometimes the wind really blew across the plains. I rode into camp about dark and Cookie had supper ready. I saw Al sitting over to the side eating.

"Howdy, Al. How is your shoulder?"

"It's ok. Just a little sore is all."

"You should ride with Cookie for a couple of days and take it easy. Give it a little time to heal."

"No, I will be ok. I can do my work."

"I still think you should lay off a couple of days. You need to be healed just in case we get in to it with someone else."

"Whatever you say, Wil."

I ate and lie looking at the stars and the moon. The coyotes were really loud. I knew they were there the other nights but I must not have paid them any mind. Their howling must have put me to sleep. All of the sudden, I felt something shaking me.

"Wil, wake up. It's time to get on the way. Here's a plate for you."

"What happened? They were supposed to wake me for watch."

"Jake felt like we didn't need the extra person on watch last night, so he let you sleep. He is already gone out this morning to scout around. He said he would see you at supper."

"I better hurry. The sun will be up soon."

When I was eating my breakfast Chris came over.

"How is it going, Chris?"

He began to roll a cigarette as he had done when we first saw him.

"Ok, sir. I'm just wondering, where are y'all from?"

He lit the cigarette as he waited for me to answer.

"Chris, we are from a little town in Texas named Lost Creek. This herd belongs to the Silver Spur Ranch."

"I've heard of Lost Creek, but I haven't heard of the Silver Spur Ranch."

"Other ranches near there are bigger. That may be why you haven't heard of it."

"Maybe. I best get out with the herd."

"Ok, Chris, I'll talk with you later."

Chris was a tall, slender person. I didn't realize how tall he was until just then. He looked like he would have been good with a gun. I just hoped we didn't have to find out. I handed my plate to Cookie and saddled Dobbs.

CHAPTER EIGHT

It looked like it was going to be another nice day. I could see the sun just barely peeking up. The birds were beginning to stir around. I just couldn't believe how loud they were sometimes. We were getting close to the Canadian River. We had been moving slower the past few days. After we crossed the Canadian River, it would be a few days to Camp Supply. Cookie would be able to restock the chuck wagon when we got there. We trailed the herd heading north and a little west. Toward the end of the day I saw a man headed in our direction from the north. When he got closer, I saw that it was Jake.

"How's it going, Wil?"

"Ok, Jake. It's been a nice, easy day."

"Good. We'll be at the Canadian River sometime in the morning. It's running pretty full but I think we will be able to cross ok."

"Did you see any sign of the Indians?"

"No, wasn't any sign of them today."

"Good, maybe we are through with them."

We pushed the cattle until almost dark, then rode into camp. Cookie had fixed something to eat. We talked as we ate, then turned in for the night. The critters were sure making noise. I fell asleep listening to them, as they seem to harmonize. Cookie had us going early, as usual. We got out with the herd and began to drive toward the Canadian River. About midmorning we approached the Canadian River. With it so full we couldn't tell where the banks were, which made it hard to cross.

"Well Jake, where do you think we will be able to cross?"

"I think we should be able to cross just to the east of here."

"Ok, Jake. Let's turn the herd and head that way."

I whistled and pointed toward the east. The men nodded and we began to move the cattle east. Jake was heading toward the bank of the river where he thought we could cross. Cookie headed the chuck wagon in that direction. When Cookie got to the river, he found a gentle slope to take the wagon down. When he reached the edge of the river, the horses begin to sink in the sand.

Cookie yelled, "Jake, quicksand!"

"Wil, we have trouble. Hold the cattle up over there and get some of the boys over here with their lassos!"

I turned and yelled.

"Hold up. Tom, Chris, Dan, get your lassos and come over to the wagon. There's trouble!"

When we reached the wagon, Jake had his lasso on one of the horses. I put my lasso on the other one. They were fighting the sand with all their strength. They were jumping and jerking and all the time, they were screaming a blood-curdling scream. Their teeth seemed to grind and their nostrils flared between screams. Their eyes were wide and glaring. I knew they were just terrified of being in that sand. I heard horses scream in such a way when they came on a rattlesnake, but it was not near like that. Tom, Chris, and Dan put their lasso on the wagon to try to pull it back.

"Ok, boys, lets give it a try and pull all at once. Now!"

When Jake gave the order, we all began to pull. The wagon was coming out of the sand but we couldn't get the horses to move. I guess they were just too deep.

"Cookie, undo whatever you can get to on the harness. We will have to let the horses go. They are just too deep to get out."

"Ok, Jake."

He began to climb down on the horse's backs, which was out of the sand. It was hard for him to stay on their backs with them jumping around. Once he had the harness loose, I shot the horses so they wouldn't suffer any longer. We could easily get the wagon up then.

Cookie yelled, "Pull now, boys!"

Chris repeated the order and they began to pull the wagon out of the sand. Cookie was safely on the wagon as we pulled it up the bank of the river. The horses were totally gone in the sand.

"I never expected to have quicksand here, Wil. I guess I should have been a little more observant."

"We're ok, Jake. Don't beat yourself up over it. We can replace the horses. We'll just find another place to cross."

"You're right, Wil. I feel like I didn't do my job."

We held the cattle off the river while we looked for another place to cross. I went downstream along the river and Jake went upstream. Jake found another place, which didn't take long.

"Over here, Wil."

I rode over to where Jake was and we looked it over. Jake decided he would go through and test it before we took the cattle through.

"You didn't have anything to prove, Jake."

"Sure I did. I didn't want anything else to go into quicksand or the river."

Jake continued across the river and I motioned the boys to move the herd. It was a slow process, but we finally had the herd across the river. By the time we were across the river it was mid afternoon. Cookie found the extra rigging and Dan rounded up some horses from the Remuda. Everyone was safely across and the wagon seemed to have floated most of the way. Rather than stopping to eat, we pushed on until about dark. After we had the herd settled for the night, I met Jake at camp. I stepped over and talked to Jake away from everyone else.

"Jake, you didn't have anything to prove back there. With so many places along the river that could have spots like that, we hit one. It's no one's fault. You did your job."

"That may be, Wil, but I still should have seen it."

"I could have missed it as easily as you did. Don't worry about it."

"Ok, Wil. Tomorrow is a new day. Maybe we can go without any problems."

"Yeah, I think we have had our share of them already, Jake."

We had our meal, which wasn't much because some of the things on the wagon had gotten wet and ruined. Cookie made due with what he had. He would have to replace those things at Camp Supply.

"Jake, I think I will bring in some wild game tomorrow so we'll have some fresh meat."

"I think that'll be good, Wil."

Before I turned in for the evening, I told Cookie my plan. He thought it sounded like a good idea. Morning came too soon, but we got around and headed out once again. I was on the lookout for some game. I would have liked to have a deer, but I'd settle for any-thing. I was able to get several rabbits and a couple of pheasant. That would be enough to make a good stew or something. I took the game over to Cookie for him to fix, but when I arrived at the wagon I found that Jake had brought in a small deer.

"Cookie, I was afraid that what I was able to

find wouldn't be enough, but with this deer we should have plenty."

"Yeah, Wil, I should have plenty for another meal, also."

"Jake, I looked all day for a deer and here you come in with one. Where did you come across one?"

"I just happened to run on it in a creek bottom north of here. It was just standing there grazing."

"I'm just glad you did, Jake. Well, the herd is a few miles back, so I guess I'll go see about helping get them here for the night."

"Hold on, Wil. I'll be right with you."

We continued to push the herd. Close to camp we got the cattle settled for the night. I couldn't wait to get in and have some venison. I had that on my mind all day after Jake brought in that deer. We headed in, and I took care of Dobbs and headed for something to eat.

"I'm ready for some of that venison, Cookie."

"Here you go, Wil. Coffee, too?"

"Sure, Cookie. Thanks."

I sat by the fire to eat and visit with some of the boys. The weather had not changed much since we started. The nights were still cool even though we had been on the trail for several weeks. The days seemed to get a little warmer. A few more days and we would be at Camp Supply. I knew after that river-crossing Cookie needed a lot of things in the wagon. What didn't get lost was thrown out because it had gotten wet.

One of the boys was playing a little tune on a mouth harp. I fell asleep listening to the tune he was playing.

I was awakened by Cookie banging pots and pans. He was not happy about something. This was not like him at all. I got up, walked over to where he was, and asked him about his troubles.

"Cookie, what's wrong?"

"Oh, I don't have what I need to fix anything the way I want to. We just lost so much in the river."

"Don't worry about fixing things just right. Just fix what you have. The boys will understand. They know what we went through at the river."

"Maybe so, Wil. I just get a little frustrated trying to fix things."

"It's ok. We'll make do."

I got some coffee and sat back down.

CHAPTER NINE

The wind was blowing out of the northwest that morning. The air felt a little damp. I couldn't tell if there were any clouds. I hoped we didn't have rain all day. I was hearing a rumbling that sounded like horses coming from a distance. Then it clicked in my mind that the sound must be Indians or thieves running toward us.

"Get your guns, boys. We may be in for a fight. Dan, head to the herd and warn the others that we may have a fight coming."

"I'm on my way, Wil."

"Cookie, you still have that rifle in the wagon? You better get it."

The sound of horses got louder as they came closer. Jake got on his horse and headed out so he might get around behind them. We didn't have much cover if there was shooting. We used the wagon, some rocks, and the brush close by for cover. Since it was still dark, we moved out away from the fire Cookie had going so they wouldn't be able to see us as well. We were ready for whatever was coming in. All at once they were there. About twenty or thirty Indians were upon us. They were running through the camp, guns blazing. They must have gotten enough guns and ammunition from other raids. They had as much firepower as we did. I shot three of them as they passed me. I looked toward the wagon and I saw an Indian coming in behind Cookie.

"Cookie, look out behind you!"

The Indian fell from my shot, but it was too late. He had already gotten Cookie. I ran over to check on him, shooting wildly as the Indians continued to run through camp. When I reached him he appeared to be dead.

"Cookie! Cookie!"

His hand seemed lifeless and I didn't get any response. I continued to shoot back at the Indians. I saw Jake across from me. He had come in after hitting them from behind. He looked ok and he was shooting at those who were coming our way. It was all over in just minutes, but it felt like a lifetime. The smoke and smell from the gunpowder filled the air. The dust from all the commotion had not yet settled. A lot of Indians lay dead on the ground. The rest of the Indians took off with what horses they could. I looked around for some of the boys to be dead. We were fortunate. I just saw some wounded. I decided to go over and check on Cookie again. When I walked over where Cookie was lying, Jake saw where I was headed and joined me.

"Do you think he's dead, Wil?"

"I don't know, Jake. When I checked on him

a while ago, I didn't get a response from him, and he seemed lifeless."

Jake knelt down to check Cookie as I stood over him watching. He picked up his hand and checked for some signs of life.

"Cookie! Cookie!"

Jake called his name, but there didn't appear to be any signs of life. Then we heard a muffled moan. He began to move some. Once he became fully conscious, we figured out what had happened. He was shot; it threw him back into the wagon wheel, and knocked him out. With him bleeding and not moving, he appeared to be dead.

"Thank God you're not dead, Cookie! We really thought we had lost you there for a minute."

"What's the matter, Wil? Think you were going to have to do all the cooking?"

"No, that's not it at all. You're my friend."

He laughed, and then Jake joined him. He just had to get one on me again.

"Ha, ha. That's not very funny."

Chris walked up and looked at Cookie.

"Cookie, you ok?"

"Yeah, I'm ok. Y'all just patch me up and I'll be as good as new."

"I thought we had lost him, Chris."

"Wil, if we had lost him you would still have a cook. I've done some cooking in the past."

"Good. You can patch him up and help him fix some meals until he's better."

"I don't need anyone helping me. I'll do just fine, Wil."

"Nonsense, Cookie. He can help for a while, just so you don't overdo it while you recuperate."

"Well, ok, Wil. Just for a short time, then he's back to pushing cattle."

"That suits you, Chris?"

"Sure Wil, as long as he is fine with it."

"Ok, lets get our wounded patched up and find our horses."

We saw a few of our horses close by. Jake found his horse rather quickly and headed out to find some of the others. I helped Chris with the wounded. It was almost the middle of the day. We had the wounded taken care of, and Chris was fixing a short lunch so we could get on our way. He got a little resistance from Cookie, but I think it was to let Chris know whose chuck wagon it was. Jake headed back in. He tied his horse up at the wagon and got a cup of coffee.

"Chris, this is pretty good coffee."

"Thanks, Jake."

"Wil, I can't find Dobbs anywhere. I have looked everywhere."

"Boy, I hate to lose that horse. He's been a good one."

"Wil, it looks as though we may have just enough horses left. They got off with quite a few. Some of the boys are still looking for horses as they round up cattle that have strayed. Maybe they'll find Dobbs."

We grabbed something to eat, and had just finished when the other boys rode in. They had a few more of the horses with them, but not Dobbs.

"Well, I guess I'll have to make due with another horse."

We were a few saddles short, so some of us rode with just a blanket or bareback. I preferred to ride bareback. When we were packing up and getting ready to move out, I saw a horse coming in from a distance. When it got closer, it looked like Dobbs. He evidently got loose from the Indians.

"Look, Wil. It's Dobbs!"

"Yeah, Jake. I'm sure glad to have him back."

"Wil, I think I'm going to track this bunch of Indians and see if I can get some of the horses back. I'll try to catch you by the time you get to Camp Supply, if everything goes ok."

"Ok, Jake. I'll keep the herd moving that direction. You be careful. This is a wild bunch we are dealing with."

"I'll be ok, Wil. Don't worry about me. Just get the herd north."

We watched him ride out to the west, and we got the herd on the move. I was thinking about how we almost lost Cookie, and I had a sinking feeling in my gut. Just the thought of losing a good friend made me sick to my stomach. About that time, Slim rode up.

"What is the matter, Wil? You look as though you've seen a ghost."

"I'm ok, Slim. Must be something I ate."

Having mentioned that it was something I had eaten made me remember we were low on food.

I thought since we were still about two days out from Camp Supply and low on supplies, I would try to get some game for supper tonight. We could see how good of a cook Chris really was.

I began to look for game as we pushed the herd to keep my mind off of what went on that morning. Although, I would never forget what happened. I had forgotten about the air feeling damp. When I was looking around, it was somewhat cloudy, but didn't look like it would rain. Since we were slowed down by the events that morning, we still would be able to make Wolf Creek by nightfall. I saw a large deer feeding in a little low spot with some tall grass. I took careful aim so that I didn't miss. I got him! When I headed over to get the deer I saw some kind of large cat headed for him. I pulled my rifle and shot at him. The first shot missed. I took careful aim and the second shot got him. When I reached the place where the cat was, I saw it was a mountain lion. You didn't see many of them in those parts. I retrieved my deer and took it to Chris.

"Here, Chris. This should be good for supper tonight. You don't mind cleaning him, do you?"

"No, not at all. I'll get right on it so it can bleed out along side the wagon, until we get to camp."

"Ok, see you in a few hours."

We pushed on, and the sun was getting low in the sky. I thought about Jake being out there looking for the Indians. I just hoped he was ok. I saw Wolf Creek just ahead with a big spot for the cattle to graze along the bank. I rode back to the herd and told them where we would bed them down.

"Ok, boys. Bed them down just ahead in the grass near Wolf Creek."

It was almost dark. I was worn out but I didn't know if I would be able to sleep worrying about another attack. I headed into camp where Chris had supper ready.

"Chris, something sure smells good."

"Here you go, Wil."

When I got the plate from Chris, I grabbed a cup and he filled it with coffee. I took my plate out away from the fire a little ways and sat down. I tried what Chris had fixed.

"Chris, this is pretty good."

Cookie chimed in about what I said.

"His cooking is pretty good, huh? Well he may just have to cook all the time if you don't like my cooking."

"Cookie, I didn't say I didn't like yours. I just was commenting on Chris' cooking. I don't think you have anything to worry about. Chris doesn't want to cook all the time, any more then you want to push cattle."

"Ok Wil, I see your point."

"You will be back to cooking all the time before you know it. Here you go, Chris."

I handed Chris my plate and got another cup of coffee. I sure hoped the Indians didn't attack us again. Maybe Jake would be ok.

CHAPTER TEN

T he next couple of days went uneventful as we were just outside Camp Supply.

"Boys, keep 'em close and on this grazing. We have to go over to Camp Supply and get some things."

"Ok, Wil. Get us some tobacco if they have any."

"Sure, Slim. I'll check. Cookie, did you give Chris a list of things you needed to get?"

"Yeah. I still don't know why I shouldn't go."

"I was just thinking that you should rest your wound. You should go if you don't think the shoulder will bother you too much."

"Wil, I'll be ok and Chris will be there to help with the supplies."

"Ok, let's move out. You ready, Chris?"

"Yep," Chris said.

In about a half hour or so we would be at Camp Supply. The Army from Camp Supply rode up as we were getting ready to go.

"Howdy, Lieutenant. I'm Wil Gannon. What brings you out here?"

"Colonel Brown sent us to escort you."

"We could have used you boys some time back when we were raided by Indians."

"We heard y'all was on the way but we had more pressing matters to attend to before we could join you."

"Lieutenant, we are on our way to Camp Supply to pick up some things we need. I also need to speak to the Colonel about getting some saddles and tack for some our horses."

"Mr. Gannon, we'll be happy to escort you there and we'll leave some of our detail here to assist if there is any trouble."

"That sounds good. We're ready to leave now so we can be back to the herd before it gets late."

"Corporal, you take half the men with you and help watch the herd. The other half, forward ho," the Lieutenant said.

The three of us rode in front of the command with the Lieutenant. We all made light conversation while we had our ride to Camp Supply. We told of our run in with the Indians and the twister that we had seen. We could see Camp Supply from a long way out, just a rustic outpost for the soldiers.

"Chris, you take Cookie to the mercantile and I am going to have the Lieutenant take me to see Colonel Brown."

"Ok, Wil. I'll meet up with you later."

I rode over to one of the better buildings in the compound with the Lieutenant. Although there wasn't much difference from the other buildings, this one had some of the extras. A large man came out of the structure as we approached. He was in uniform and he was wearing a hat. He must have been about six-feet tall with a mustache and chin whiskers that seemed almost gray. The Lieutenant saluted and announced my name when we were in front of the Colonel.

"Colonel Brown, this is Wil Gannon, trail boss from the herd that has been coming our way."

"Mr. Gannon, get down from your horse and come in for some coffee."

"I would be happy to, Colonel."

I climbed down from Dobbs and followed the colonel into the structure he had been standing in front of. It was pretty rustic, but it didn't have the gaps in the walls the way the other ones had. The floors were dirt and in some places it looked as though there were some weeds or something growing. He reached over, got some cups, and went to a stove that had a coffee pot. He filled the cups and handed one to me.

"Thanks, Colonel."

"Our detail was supposed to meet you and your herd sooner. We were on the trail of a rustler, William A. Hudman—sometimes known as Coonskin Bill—his associate, John Wild Horse, and his gang. Coonskin Bill is a big man and rides a black stallion. John Wild Horse is a half breed that rides a paint."

"That's the men the Rangers were looking for back in Texas. I think they hit us once on the trail and we lost them. They managed to get a few head of cattle.

We had a feeling they were ahead of us all the way, but didn't know where they were."

"We lost them as well, Mr. Gannon."

"I just hope we don't have a run in with them on our way to Dodge City."

"That is one of the reasons we have a detail that is going with you. Is there anything else that I can do for you, Mr. Gannon?"

"Yes, Colonel. Indians hit us and we are in need of some saddles and some tack. I think we can get everything else that we need from the mercantile."

"I think we can round up some saddles for you, Mr. Gannon, and whatever else you might need as well. I'll have the Lieutenant load what you need in your wagon."

"Colonel, I am prepared to trade you some cattle for what we need. Do you think a few head of cattle are fair trade?"

"Mr. Gannon, I think that sounds more than fair."

"I will sure be glad to get to Dodge City with this herd and have it done."

"I'm looking forward to going to Dodge City soon myself. My wife is there because I don't want her to live in these conditions. Maybe you will see her there. Mrs. Joyce Brown is her name. She is a little over five feet tall and has blonde hair. She lives in the boarding house near the train yard."

"I'll be sure to tell her if I see her that you send your best and can't wait to see her."

"That would be fine, Mr. Gannon. Y'all have a

good trip. The dispatch will accompany you about half the distance to Dodge City from here. Another dispatch from Dodge City should meet up with you, then escort you the rest of the way."

"Thanks, Colonel, I hope you get to see your wife soon."

I turned and walked out the door to meet up with Cookie and Chris. When I started to mount Dobbs, Jake rode up.

"Howdy, Jake. Sure glad you made it. I was worried you might have trouble with those Indians."

"I tracked them for a long way but I didn't catch up with them. Then I lost their tracks. That is when I decided to just catch up with the herd and let it go."

"Colonel Brown has agreed to trade some saddles and some tack for a few head of cattle."

"That's good, Wil."

"I was just about to get Cookie and Chris and head on back to the herd."

I climbed on Dobbs and we rode around to the mercantile. Just as we rode up, Chris was loading the last of the supplies. I saw the saddles and other tack had been loaded. The Lieutenant and his detail rode up.

"Mr. Gannon, we are ready to escort you back to your herd."

"We are ready to go, Lieutenant."

We returned to the herd and trailed the cattle the rest of the day. The Lieutenant had half the detail ahead of the herd and the other half trailing the herd. About another day and we would be in Kansas.

The air was getting cold as it got dark and the

wind was out of the north. I would have thought it was too late in the year for cold weather, but we didn't know what the weather was going to do sometimes. We settled into camp and invited the detail to join us for meals. They were more than happy to because they were not looking forward to having a cold meal from their saddlebags. After a good night's sleep we loaded up and headed north into the cold wind.

"Jake, I hope this cold air doesn't last long. I am not ready for much more of winter-like weather."

"I'm sure it won't last long, Wil."

Sure enough, later that afternoon, the wind changed and it began to warm some.

"Well, we'll be in Kansas by dark and the detail will head back to Camp Supply tomorrow."

"I just hope the other detail out of Dodge City will be here before long."

"Wil, if Colonel Brown said they would be here then they probably will be."

"You never know what kind of trouble they may run into and have to take care of first."

"That's true enough, Wil. We'll just have to take it one day at a time. Besides, we took care of things without them before. We can do it again."

"Yeah, but it is nice to have them around."

"Having the Army around is nice because we have extra guns if something happens."

"Jake, do you mind if I ask a personal question?"

"I don't know, Wil, I guess it depends on the question."

"Well, do you believe there is a power other than man that makes things happen, and that things happen for a reason?"

I no sooner got it out of my mouth and the Lieutenant rode up.

"Jake, I would like you to accompany me ahead to scout around."

"Sure, Lieutenant. Wil, I'll get back to you on that question."

I rode over to the wagon and checked on Cookie. I would imagine that his wound still hurt plenty.

"Howdy, Chris. Howdy, Cookie. How is that gunshot doing?"

"Wil, it's healing up ok but it's still pretty sore."

"I think you should take it easy for a little while longer. We have Chris here to help out and he doesn't mind. Do you, Chris?"

"No, not at all, Wil. I kind of enjoy the break from the herding. Wil, do you think we are in Kansas yet?"

"No, Chris. I thought we would be there tonight but we didn't get as far as I had hoped. When we get to the Cimarron River we will be in Kansas."

"I thought there would be a river to cross, but I don't get this far north very often. I generally stay in Texas and the New Mexico Territory."

Chris handed the reins to Cookie. He rolled a cigarette and lit it in one flowing movement. I think it would have taken me that long to get tobacco out of my pocket. I hadn't ever smoked so I didn't know much about rolling a smoke.

"I better get back to the herd. I'll see you boys in camp."

I turned and rode a few miles back. Looking at the herd, I noticed it sure looked like they really had put on the weight. They should bring a good price. When I was riding around looking at the herd, Slim rode over.

"Howdy, Slim. How are we doing?"

"Pretty good, Wil. How is Cookie doing?"

"He is doing ok. Just a little sore still yet."

"That's good. Well it doesn't look like we are going to make Kansas tonight."

"No, we didn't get as far as I hoped we would, but we will be in Kansas tomorrow."

"I will be glad to see Dodge City. I am getting tired. I think the other boys are getting pretty tired, too."

"Yeah, Slim. I think they are, too. In a few days it will be all over, and you boys can rest up in Dodge and have some fun."

"Yep, that sounds mighty good to me, Wil."

"Well, let's get these things bedded down for the night" said Wil.

The next morning the Lieutenant had his men ready for return to Camp Supply.

"Good morning, Wil. We're headed back to Camp Supply today. The scout came in last night and said the troops from Dodge are about a day's ride out, and will escort you the rest of the way."

"Thanks, Lieutenant. I appreciate you being here for us and wish you a safe journey back to Camp Supply."

The Lieutenant turned and gave the order for his troops.

"Troops, mount up. Form up in twos. Forward, ho."

CHAPTER ELEVEN

I didn't think we were going to have any problems without them for a while. After all, we came a long way just the boys and the herd. Jake left out during the afternoon to scout ahead. He said he would be back sometime later that day. Meanwhile, we were going to have to cross the Cimarron River. I hoped it was not running very full. That time of the year, it could be overflowing its banks. It was not quite sun up, but we were going to have to be moving out soon. After some of Chris's breakfast, we would be on our way.

"Chris, I am ready to have some of that breakfast."

I finished breakfast and saddled Dobbs. The sun was just beginning to show some light.

"Ok, boys. Let's get started."

We pushed the herd all morning, and about noon we were coming up to the Cimarron River. When we reached the river, Jake met us there.

"Howdy, Jake. I guess we are ready to cross this river. This a good place to cross?"

"Yep, just a little ways over to the west should be fine. It doesn't seem to be as full as some of the other rivers we crossed back in the Oklahoma Territory."

"That's good news. I wasn't wanting to cross another wild river."

I rode over and indicated to the boys to move them west some. Jake moved to the crossing place and was waiting there. Cookie and Chris were there crossing with the wagon. I watched and waited for them to cross. The water swirled around the wagon but it didn't seem very deep. The water was just below the bed of the wagon. I worried that there might be another problem. They crossed without any trouble. I waved the boys on across. After the herd had passed I began to cross. The water was very cold. Dobbs struggled with it at first, then went right on in. It was a good thing it was still early in the day and we had plenty of sun. We would be able to dry out well before dark. I decided to remain at the back of the herd to help keep strays rounded up. That was a tough job sometimes because the cattle had a mind of their own. We were bedding the herd down at a water hole, full from spring rains, when the Army from Dodge rode in. The Lieutenant dispatched some of his men with the herd and the others went into camp.

"Well, that's got them settled for the night boys. I'll be at camp if y'all need me."

"Ok, Wil. We'll see you up there later."

"Yeah, see you later, Al."

I rode over to camp. I could smell the grub that

Chris had fixed. It really did smell pretty good. I didn't say much because I didn't want to make Cookie mad.

"Howdy, Chris. Howdy, Cookie. It smells like you have supper ready."

"Yep, I sure do, Wil. You ready for a plate?"

"Yeah, I think I am, Chris."

"Here you go, Wil. Howdy, Jake, I didn't even see you. I'll get you a plate."

"I'll get some coffee while you dish it up."

"Lieutenant, you and your men help yourself. There is plenty of food."

"Thanks. I'm Lieutenant Darnell."

"I'm Wil Gannon and this is Jacob Norton."

"Wil, how is it?"

"It's pretty good food, Jake. Don't be too loud about your comments. I don't want to make Cookie mad."

"Yeah, I know what you mean. He is a little touchy about that. Ya know, Wil, I am going to be kind of sad that this drive is over in a few days. Even though it's been tiring, I have enjoyed your company. I have missed that over the last couple of years."

"Yeah, I know what you mean, Jake. Nice just having your company."

"Wil, I don't know when I'll see you again after this drive. I have taken a job driving another herd when we get back. After that, I don't know what I will be doing or where I'll be."

"You know where I'll be, Jake. So if you're ever over that way, you can always drop by and catch up again."

"Yeah, I suppose that would be good."

"I think I am going to get some rest now, Jake. Good night."

"I'm going to stay up a while. Sleep well."

I was awakened with the rattling of pots and pans again. Seemed Cookie was upset with Chris. Chris headed for his horse.

"I'm going back to the herd. I'm tired of this now anyway."

"Good, I feel well enough I can do my own cooking."

I guess that settled that argument. We pushed the cattle a few more days with the Army escort and we were in sight of Dodge City. I could tell that the boys were getting excited about the drive being over, having some fun in town, and sleeping in a real bed for a change. When we approached town, we herded the cattle to a street that was the shortest route to the stockyard. You could see some folks lining the street to watch us come in. The man at the stockyard had the gate opened for us and was counting cattle as they went by. When the last of the herd was in the yard, I rode over to talk to Jake and the Lieutenant.

"Thanks for the escort, Lieutenant. We will be seeing you around."

"You're welcome, Mr. Gannon."

"Well, Jake, while you settle up with the yardman, I'm going to the hotel to get a room."

"Ok, Wil. I'll see you later and we can eat."

I rode just up the street to the hotel nearby, but it seemed different than I remembered. I climbed down from Dobbs and headed in. The desk clerk turned to me.

"Yes, Sir. Can I help you?"

"Yeah, I would like a room and a bath."

I heard two shots ring out. A crowd began to gather down the street near the stockyards. I turned and ran out the hotel and down the street to where the crowd was gathering. The smoke from the guns was still thick in the air and the dust had not settled from the horses that had rode off. When I pushed my way through the crowd, I could see that it was Jake. Tears began to well up in my eyes and stream down my cheeks. I knelt down beside him.

"It's ok, Jake. You're going to be ok. The doctor is on the way."

"Wil, you know that question that you asked me the other day? It's yes."

"What do you mean, Jake?"

It looked bad. He could barely talk. It was more like a whisper, but I heard him just the same. Blood was pouring out of his gut, and bubbles of blood were coming from the wound in his chest. There was blood in the corner of his mouth and running out his nose. His hand was still on his gun. He had not been able to draw it to protect himself.

"Wil, you stop driving cattle and go back to Texas. Court that fine young lady in Lost Creek that Cookie was telling me about."

"Jake, who did this?"

"A rustler by the name of Coonskin Bill. He got

off with all the money from the herd. He said it is easier to let us bring them in and take the money from us."

"That's the one Colonel Brown was telling us about."

"Yeah, that's the one. His partner, Wild Horse was here with him. He's the one who distracted me, and Coonskin Bill Shot me."

"Wil, I want you to have my horse and all my things"

"Don't talk that way, Jake. You are going to be ok."

"I don't think so, Wil. I feel real cold. I have never felt this way before."

I knew it was not manly for me to cry, but I couldn't stop the tears from streaming down my cheeks. I knew in my gut he was not going to make it because it was really bad. The doc pushed through the crowd and knelt down on the other side of Jake. He looked at his wounds and just shook his head. Jake looked me right in the eyes.

"I got your back, Wil."

He was gone. Someone began to tell the crowd to disperse. He said it was all over now. How could they have known it was all over? He had just passed away. When he had made his way up to where we were, it was Marshal Deger. The assistant marshal came up behind him. Chris and some of the boys followed the marshal.

"What happened here?"

"My good friend, Jacob Norton, was mur-dered and robbed by two wanted men. Their names are

William A. Hudman, sometimes known as Coonskin Bill, and his partner is John Wild Horse."

"How do you know these are the men that did this?"

"He told me who they were before he died."

"We had received a wire about these men, but we didn't know they were in the area."

People that had been there when Jake was shot spoke up and said they heard it as well. Some time that afternoon, the marshal got a posse together and they headed out to look for those men. Chris and the boys went with the posse. I wanted to go, but someone had to make sure Jake was well taken care of. The undertaker had come up not long after the marshal left. I assisted him with Jake so that we could get him off the street. When we were at the undertaker's office, I gathered anything of real value.

"I'm Wil Gannon. I'll take care of any expense. I would like a marker for his grave, and this is what I would like on it."

I handed him a note that had how I wanted the inscription to read. I then walked out and down the street to get Jake's horse and other things. I took his horse and mine to the livery.

"Take care of these horses for me. Give them a curry and some grain. I'll be in town a few days."

"Ok, mister."

I gathered up my things along with Jake's and headed for the hotel where I was before it all started. When I walked in, the clerk recognized me and got me the key for the room he had assigned to me earlier. I turned around and there was a lady standing there.

"Howdy, ma'am."

"Did I hear you and your friend talk about Colonel Brown just before your friend died?"

"Yes ma'am. We stopped at the fort on our way up here, and he was telling us about those killers and thieves."

"Colonel Brown is my husband. How is he?"

"He is just fine, ma'am. He told us to say hello if we were to run into you here. Mrs. Brown, I'm Wil Gannon. My friend out there that just died was Jacob Norton."

I turned back to the clerk.

"Up the stairs, down the hall, and to the left. The room faces the street."

"Thanks. That'll be fine."

I picked up the key, headed up the stairs, and made my way into the room. I felt drained. I put the things I had down on a table across the room and headed for the bed. It was nice to be on a bed for a change. I hadn't been there long and I was out.

I was awakened the next morning by a knock on the door. When I opened the door, Marshal Deger was standing there.

"Wil Gannon?"

"Yeah."

"We spoke yesterday after the shooting. We searched for those two, but we lost their trail just before dark. The assistant marshal and some of your boys are going back today, to try and pick up the trail again. These guys seem to be pretty smart."

"Yeah, we dealt with them some on the trail when we were driving the cattle up from Texas. They always managed to give us the slip."

"If there is anything new to tell you, Mr. Gannon, I'll let you know right away."

"Thanks, Marshal."

I closed the door and turned to see the things I had set on the table the day before–my saddlebags and Jake's, our pistols and rifles, and bed rolls. My pistol was a Colt Navy thirty-six caliber. I noticed that Jake's was a Remington forty-four caliber. I had a Winchester forty-four rifle. The one that Jake had on his saddle was a Henry forty-four. I never knew what Jake carried. It didn't really matter. We weren't gun fighters. I looked over at Jake's saddlebags. I didn't know if it was right to go through his things just yet. When I pulled the saddle-bags over in front of me I saw the letters JN tooled on the flap. After looking at it for some time, I decided not to look in it. I went to the washstand over to one side of the door. I poured some water from the pitcher into the basin and washed my face. When I looked in the mirror in front of me, I looked rough. I needed a bath and a shave. I headed downstairs for a bath. After I was cleaned up, I walked across the street to the barbershop.

"Howdy. I would like a shave."

"Yes, sir. Would you like your haircut, too?"

I looked in the mirror in front of me. I did need it trimmed.

"Yeah, why not. It looks pretty rough."

"Ok, mister."

He began to cut. I sat there thinking about all that had gone on. I just could not believe that Jake was dead. We had just talked about how good it was to be together again. Now he was gone. He was gone for good. I hadn't thought about burying my friend. I figured we would live forever. A person doesn't think about dying.

"Mister, is there anything wrong?"

I came out of the trance I must have been in. The barber was finished and wondered why I just sat there.

"No, there's not anything wrong. I was just thinking, I guess. Sorry. Here's what I owe you."

I got my hat and walked out. I looked down the street at the spot where it all took place. Chris and some of the others rode up while I'm standing there.

"Wil, are you ok?"

"Yeah, Chris. I'm just looking around. Tell the other boys we are going to bury Jake this afternoon about an hour before sundown. They will probably want to pay their last respects."

"Ok, Wil."

I made my way back to the hotel. I was getting hungry but I didn't know if I could eat. I sat in one corner with my back to the wall. I wanted to be able to see who came and went. I don't remember having done this before, but it felt right to do it.

"Can I get you anything, sir?"

"I'll have some coffee for now."

I didn't know if that emptiness I felt in my

stomach was hunger or the loss of my friend. I finished my coffee.

"I'll have something to eat now."

"What would you like, sir?"

"I'll have a steak."

"Right away, sir."

He had that steak out in no time and filled my coffee cup. After I had eaten, I did feel somewhat better, as it had been quite a while since I had eaten. I had some more coffee and watched people passing the hotel. The shooting of Jake on the street had not meant anything to them because it was just another day to them. I suppose if I had not known him I would be the same way. Another thought came to me as I was sitting there. I didn't have any of the money from the herd to pay the boys. I knew the money I started out with for expenses wouldn't have been enough. Those boys deserved their pay. They earned it. Jake's horse and saddle could be sold, but that wouldn't have been near enough. I had decided I'd go to my room and think about what to do.

When I entered my room, I saw Jake's things on the table. I thought it might be ok to see what was in his saddlebags. When I opened one side, I saw a worn black book. I removed it from the saddlebag and opened the front cover. Just inside was a note that read, "If you have this, it means that I'm dead. So do what you wish with my things." It was signed "Jake." Under the note was some money. When I counted it, I found that it was enough to pay the boys their money and some left over. The worn book was a Bible. I didn't know Jake knew about such things as God or the Bible.

CHAPTER TWELVE

Jake said the answer to my question was yes, but I didn't remember a question. I sat on the windowsill to think on that, and just generally daydream. A knock on the door stirred me out of the trance. When I walked to the door, not thinking about the time of day, I wondered whom it could be. Cookie and Slim were there.

"Wil, are you ready to head to the cemetery?"

"Oh, yeah. I guess we better go. It's getting late."

I must have sat on that windowsill longer than I thought. I got my hat and went down the stairs after the boys. We met in the hotel lobby and headed out for the cemetery together. The cemetery was not far. When we got closer, some of the other boys joined us. Nobody said anything on the way. When we were finally at the cemetery, it felt like it had taken forever to get there. The undertaker was waiting for us at a gravesite where a wooden box was sitting. A preacher was there by his side.

"Howdy, boys. Wil, I asked the preacher here to say a few words. Is that ok?"

"Sure. I think Jake would have liked that."

We gathered around the coffin as the preacher opened his book.

> *"The Lord is my shepherd; I shall not want. He maketh me to lie down in green pastures; he leadeth me beside the still waters. He restoreth my soul; he leadeth me in the paths of righteousness for His name's sake. Yea, though I walk through the valley of the shadow of death, I fear no evil; for thou art with me; thy rod and thy staff they comfort me. Thou preparest a table before me in the presence of mine enemies; thou anointest my head with oil; my cup runneth over. Surely goodness and mercy shall follow me all the days of my life; and I will dwell in the house of the Lord forever.*

"We commend his soul to the Lord and return his body to the earth."

The preacher turned and walked away. The undertaker and two others began to put Jake's coffin in the ground. Most of the boys left, but I remained and watched as they covered him with dirt. When they had finished, I knelt down and placed my hand on his grave.

"Jake, I swear on your grave, I will see that the two that did this will pay for their crime."

The others were just outside the cemetery.

"You boys meet me in the hotel lobby and I will get your pay. Y'all worked hard, and it's time you be paid for your work."

I went to my room and got the money from the Bible. When I paid each one, I thanked them for their work and told them I'd see them back in Texas. Chris was the last in line. I tried to hand him the money but he didn't want to take it.

"Chris, take the money. Jake would have wanted me to make sure you boys were taken care of."

"I know, Wil, but I feel bad about taking it under these circumstances."

"You take this and I won't hear any more about it."

"Ok, but let me go with you to find these guys."

"Chris, what makes you think that I am going after these guys?"

"I heard you swear on his grave that you would get the guys that did this."

"I meant that I would make sure that justice was done. That doesn't mean that I am going after them."

"I don't know much about you, Wil, but I think I know you well enough to know that you will go after these guys."

"Chris, even if I do, this is something that I would have to do by myself. I don't want you to go with me."

"Wil, you can't stop me from going to look for them on my own. I will if you don't want me to go with you."

"Chris, you do what you have to do and I'll do what I have to do."

I knew it wouldn't do any good to argue with him because he was hard headed and had a mind of his own. Maybe I could think about things up in my room and rest. When I walked into my room, I looked at the saddlebags on the table. I decided to see what else there was in them. In the side that I had taken the Bible from, there were a couple of letters, clothing, some of Cookie's biscuits, and some dried beef in a cloth bag. In the other side there was a box of cartridges for his rifle, some load for his pistol, a knife, some shaving gear, and a shirt. He had about the same things as I had for the trip. I looked at the two letters. One was from a woman, Rebecca Goldman. The other, posted some time later, was from a Mr. Goldman.

I removed the letter from Rebecca Goldman and began to read.

"My dearest Jacob,

I miss you so very much and cannot wait for your return. I have made my dress for our wedding. It is very lovely. I think you will like it very much. We'll plan on the wedding a week after your return."

The letter went on with some romantic stuff and at the bottom it was signed, "With all my love, Rebecca."

A lock of hair was in there too. Dark brown hair tied in a yellow ribbon. I returned them to the bag as they were and looked at the other letter.

"Mr. Jacob Norton,

It has come to fall upon me to tell you that

Rebecca had the fever and died. She was just too weak to pull out of it. We buried her yesterday on a hilltop under a tree here at our place. We are all terribly grieved as I'm sure you are as you read this. Mr. Goldman"

He was supposed to marry Rebecca, then got the letter from her father and it didn't happen. He had never said anything to me about that. I guess he was dealing with it the best way he knew how. The letters were dated several years back. That must have been the time he was gone from Lost Creek.

The trail was already getting cold. I wanted to catch those boys. After a short night, I woke up well before daylight. I gathered my things and headed down for breakfast. I settled up with the hotel clerk after breakfast and went down the street to the livery. I figured I'd sell Jake's horse and saddle. When I walked in the livery I saw my horse, but Jake's horse was not around. The man that runs the livery walked in.

"Where is the other horse that I left here the other day?"

"A tall slender fellow came in yesterday and said he was buying it from you and the saddle, too. He sold his horse to me and he gave me the money for the other one to give to you. He said you wouldn't mind, that you would be selling it anyway."

"I was planning to sell it, but he should have at least come to me."

"Here is the money that is due you. I took out what you owed me for the stable."

"Get my horse ready for me, please. I have to go down the street for something."

"Sure thing, Mr. Gannon."

I walked up the street to the mercantile. I decided if I was going after those boys, I needed a better side arm. The owner of the mercantile was sweeping off the walk out front.

"Howdy. I need to get a few things."

"Yes, sir. What can I get for you?"

"I need the supplies on this list."

When he began to get the things on the list, I looked at the new guns he had behind the counter. He returned.

"What else can I get for you, sir?"

"Let me see that pistol right there."

"This is a Colt Peacemaker 45."

It looked to be similar to the one I'd seen Chris carry.

"I'll take it. Let me have a couple of boxes of cartridges for it, also."

I paid him and was out to the door with my things to head for the livery. I loaded my saddlebags on Dobbs and decided to head south.

CHAPTER THIRTEEN

The first day I didn't stop until way into the night. I rode two days. Late that evening I came to a place in Kansas near no-mans land, a strip of land between Kansas and Texas.

"Howdy, I'm Wil Gannon."

"I'm Mr. Rodgers. Why don't you stay for the night? You can water your horse and I'll get some grain for him."

"Thanks, I believe I will. My horse and I are worn out. Have there been any men come through here in the past week? One would be riding a black stallion and the other is riding a paint."

"Yes, I did see a couple of men come by here on the horses you described. One is a half Indian and the other a large burly man. They said their names were John and William, I think."

"They are the ones that I am looking for."

"Why are you looking for these men?"

"They are the men that robbed and killed my

friend in Dodge City. They were able to lose the lawmen that were looking for them. I decided that I would try to find them myself and bring them in."

"When they left here they headed south. They may be headed for Mobeetie. Some call it Hidetown. That is about ninety or a hundred miles from here."

I decided to bed down in the barn and rest before I moved on. If those boys went to Mobeetie, they would stop and spend some money. I thought I'd get there before they left.

"Are you sure it's ok for me to stay for the night?"

"Yes, Mr. Gannon, and get all the water you need."

"Thanks, Mr. Rodgers. You sure are liberal with your water out here where there doesn't seem to be much."

"That's ok. I have all the water I need. See you in the morning."

"Ok, Mr. Rodgers."

I put Dobbs in a stall next to me and bedded down for the night. It was early the next morning when I woke up and decided to leave. The sun was not yet up and I didn't want to wake Mr. Rodgers. I saddled Dobbs, got plenty of water for several days and headed out. It didn't take long for me to get to no-mans land between Kansas and Texas. I continued to ride all day and into the night before I stopped to rest. Dobbs must have been tired, also. I was in Texas, and it was probably another day's ride to Mobeetie. Being back in the area where there were Indians, I worried about starting a fire. But I decided to make a small fire and have some coffee. While sitting near the fire I decided to get the Bible from my saddlebags that once belonged to Jake. There seemed to be corners turned down all through it. I wondered if he was marking the pages that way. I opened it to one of those places and found he had written on the side.

"Rules to live by."

I read down through the words and came to "*Thou shalt not kill.*" I paused there as I thought about that. I thought about what I was trying to do. I hadn't headed out on the journey to kill anyone. I just wanted to bring someone to justice for killing Jake. I thought about some of the other things I read. It went along with what I believed the Code of the West was.

My mind began to wonder back to the time of Jake's death. Seeing him lie there on the edge of life, I hadn't seen any fear in his eyes. He appeared to be at peace with everything. Then I remembered him saying that the answer to my question is yes. I went back in my mind to everything that we talked about on the trip. I just couldn't remember anything that we'd talked about that he would answer yes to. The fire began to die out and my eyes were so heavy.

I woke up early still clutching the Bible. I guess I fell asleep reading and thinking about Jake. About sunup, I gathered my things and saddled Dobbs. I was on my way just as the sun started to peek over the hills.

Riding out there with nobody around leaves you with nothing but your thoughts. It felt like I had been riding forever from one rise to the next through the sagebrush. I saw something way off in the south. When I got closer, I could see that it must be Mobeetie, which still took a long while to get there. When I rode in, I saw why they sometimes call it Hidetown. There were little hut-like places built with buffalo hides. I saw that the military had established a post there, Fort Elliott. I had heard of it but didn't know where it was. I decided to check with the military first. Maybe they had seen or heard something about Bill or John. When I approached the military post, there was a Corporal at the gate.

"Howdy, Corporal. I am Wil Gannon. Would you take me to the commander of the post?"

"Yes, Mr. Gannon. Follow me."

I followed him to one of the larger structures in the post. When we reached the front, I tied Dobbs to the rail. The Corporal led me through the door into a large military office. When he entered he saluted.

"Colonel Actkins, this is Mr. Gannon. He asked to see you sir. Mr. Gannon, this is Colonel Actkins."

"Mr. Gannon, what can I do for you?"

"Colonel, I am on the trail of two men that killed my good friend, Jacob Norton. I thought I would check to see if, by chance, you knew if they've come though here. Their names are William A. Hudman and John Wild Horse. Hudman is sometimes known as Coonskin Bill. He rides a black stallion. He is a large man. John Wild Horse rides a paint, and he is half Indian."

"I am sorry, Mr. Gannon. I haven't seen these men or heard anything about them."

"Colonel, if I may."

"Yes, Corporal."

"Colonel, I have seen horses like these in town, and some of the girls in one of the establishments said something about the big man being so obnoxious. The girls were glad when he left. They were a little afraid of him. I don't know of the half Indian man you mentioned."

"Where is this place that you are telling us about, Corporal?"

"It is on that rise just west of here. They call it Feather Hill. The lady that was glad he left is Frog Mouth Annie. You will know her when you see her. She chews tobacco. She has a big tobacco stretch in the corner of her mouth."

"Thanks, Corporal. I think I will pay her a visit and see what she knows about these two men. Colonel Actkins, thanks for your time. I just want to see that they get brought in for what they did."

"Mr. Gannon, be very careful with these two. They killed before, so they won't have a problem killing again. Maybe you should not go after them alone."

"I'll be fine, Colonel. Have a good day, sir."

I turned to walk out the door when it opened.

"Excuse me, ma'am. I was just leaving."

"Hello, Elisabeth. This is Mr. Gannon. Mr. Gannon, this is my wife, Elisabeth."

"Happy to make your acquaintance, ma'am. I must be on my way. Good day."

I mounted Dobbs and left the post. After I left, I could see the place on the rise the Corporal had told me about. When I approached the front of the place, I looked around for any sign that the two could have been in the area. I didn't see them or their horses around the place. I tied Dobbs to the post in front of the establishment. Walking across the boardwalk to the door, I heard my spurs jingle and the boards creak as I proceeded. Inside you could hear laughing and talking from men and women. When I opened the door, everyone in the room stopped and looked at me then went on with whatever they were doing. There were women sitting in men's laps, and men with their arms around some of the women at the bar. I stood there looking around the room as a nice looking lady in black satin and diamonds came up to me.

"Can I help you find something, cowboy?"

"I am looking for a lady they call Frog Mouth Annie. They told me at the fort that she might be able to tell me about two men that I am looking for."

"She is busy right now. But I'm sure she will be back in here real soon. Why don't you get yourself a drink and wait."

"Do they have coffee? I sure could use a cup right now."

"Yes, they should have some made."

I walked over to the bar and asked for some coffee. I waited and watched the people in the room. They were doing what I figured a person should do only after they are married. I guess that comes from my upbringing. I had just about finished my coffee when a woman like the one the Corporal had told me about walked up.

"Howdy, cowboy. Did you want to see me?"

"Yes, ma'am. I wanted to ask you about two men that might have come in here. One is half Indian man called John Wild Horse or just John. The other one is a tall, heavily built man. They call him Bill or William. Can you tell me anything about them, if you've seen them, and maybe something about where they might be headed?"

"The tall heavily built man was in here a few days back. The other one came up with his friend but didn't stay. He left and I guess went to one of the saloons down the way. Hey, keep your hands off."

She turned and slapped the man that had just grabbed her. He started to throw a punch and I reached up and grabbed his fist.

"Hold on there. We don't hit ladies."

He came across with the other hand and hit me squarely in the eye. He went for his gun but I didn't have time to react. Frog Mouth Annie had seen him go for his gun. She pulled her hideout gun just in time. She shot the man in the back. His gun discharged and a bullet went right beside me and across the room into the wall.

"You all right, cowboy?"

"Yeah, I just feel like I was kicked by a horse. Thanks for saving my life."

"You seem like a good person and I don't see many like you here. It would be a shame to have him kill you. Looks like that eye is going to be black for a while."

"I'll be all right, but that man is dead."

"Yeah, I get his kind in here all the time. I don't

109

kill many of them though. Hey Sam, would you clean up this mess and get him out of here?"

"Sure, Miss Annie."

"That tall heavily built man that you asked about was one of those mean ones like this guy. He came in looking for fun and paid for his time. He did slap me around a bit and was really rough. I was sure glad to see him leave."

"Did he happen to say anything about where he might be headed?"

"No, not specifically. He did comment that the girls in New Mexico were prettier and gave him a better time for his money. He said that it would not be long before he would have their company. I assume that meant he might be headed to New Mexico."

"Yeah, it sounds like that might be what he had in mind. Thanks for your time, ma'am. I must be on my way."

"Hey, why are you after these two men anyway?"

"They robbed and killed my friend, Jacob Norton. I swore on his grave that I would bring them to justice."

"I just bet you will, too. You take care of yourself, and if you're ever by here again, stop in and I'll buy you a cup coffee."

"Thanks, ma'am. I will if I am ever back this way."

There must have been a higher power in there to help save me from that bullet. Hmm. I remembered the question I asked Jake. That was why he answered yes just before he died. I had asked him if he believed there was a higher power other than that of man and if things happen for a reason. He didn't forget me asking him that question and answered me just as he was about to die. So he believed that there was a higher power that determines things. I thought of the Bible that I had found in his things. That was where he came to believe some of these things.

It was getting late. I thought I'd find a room and get an early start in the morning. I untied Dobbs and walked down the street to the livery. I left him there and I walked to the hotel that I saw just across the way. After the clerk gave me a key to my room, I went next door and got something to eat. I must have really been hungry because it didn't take me long to eat. I headed back to my room and put my things on the table just inside. I looked around the room. The hotel room was a simple room, like most of the other hotel rooms that I had been in. It had a bed, a chair, a washstand, a basin, and a pitcher. I got the little Bible out of my things and sat in the chair by the window. I figured I would read. I read through about a dozen pages until just about dark. I put it back with my things and got into bed. I didn't know when I'd get to sleep in a bed again, so I would enjoy it while I could. I fell asleep quickly, thinking about what had happened.

CHAPTER FOURTEEN

Early the next morning I was jarred by something in a dream. I got up and decided to move on. As I walked to the livery to get Dobbs, I noticed the street was empty. There didn't seem to be very many people up at that hour. I heard a few people in some of the parlors just up the street. After Dobbs was saddled, I mounted up and headed west. If those two thieves stopped on and off, I could catch up with them.

I rode all day until long after it got dark. I came to a river I think was the Canadian. I had decided it was time to rest and give Dobbs a break. We both got a drink from the river and I removed the saddle from Dobbs. He seemed to be happy about not having it on his back. I didn't take time to start a fire. I just put my bedroll down by my saddle and went fast to sleep.

I was awakened by the noise of birds with their early morning feeding and the water in the river running over some rocks. I had almost forgotten where I was. I saw Dobbs had been grazing there near the river.

I got some dried beef from my saddlebags to stave off the hunger that I was feeling and got some water from the river.

"Well, Dobbs, are you ready to head out again?"

His head moved up and down as though he were nodding as I put the saddle on. I mounted and headed west once again. It was sometime after noon when I arrived in Tascosa, Texas. I asked the local saloonkeeper about the two men, and he said they had been there. He also said they talked about business in New Mexico. I wasted no more time there and continued west. I had not gotten far from Tascosa when a few cowboys rode up. Not knowing who they were, I was ready to draw my gun at the first sign of trouble.

"Howdy, cowboy. Where are you headed?"

"Howdy, boys. I am headed to New Mexico."

"You are on the XIT Ranch here and we are employed by the ranch. They don't like just anyone on the ranch."

"Sorry, boys. I didn't know I was on anyone's property. I don't plan on being here any longer than it takes to go across. If that is ok with you boys," said Wil.

"Sure, just keep moving and you'll be ok. By the way, what is your name cowboy?"

"My name is Wil Gannon. I am on the trail of some killers. I don't think you boys would want these two on the ranch. They are rustlers and thieves. Well, I'll be on my way."

"Ok, Mr. Gannon. Good luck."

I saw herds of antelope the first few days and a

few buffalo. There were some Kiowa Indians and some Apache off in the distance. They seemed to be on the move or they were up to something unusual. They didn't seem to be in their normal routine.

It had been over a week since I left Tascosa. I knew it was going to take me longer to find them, but I could not keep up the pace the way that I was going. I would be on the Santa Fe Trail before long. Fort Union would be just before I got to the mountains. Late that afternoon I saw a rider coming from the north. I knew that everyone was not bad, but out there you just didn't know. I was ready in case there was any trouble. He rode up and I watched his hands and eyes.

"Howdy. I'm headed for Fort Union. Can you tell me if it is near here?"

"Well, cowboy, you are about a half day's ride from there. It is just north of here."

"Thanks, mister. I'll be on my way."

"Safe journey, cowboy."

I turned Dobbs to the north and once again headed for the fort. It was late in the afternoon, so I knew I wouldn't make it to the fort. I decided to make camp just after dark. It was not as cold back in Texas. I guessed the mountains had cold air coming off of them. I gathered what I could and built a fire. I just hoped the Indians didn't see the fire and decide to come check me out. I put my saddle and bedroll close to the fire and read some in the little black Bible.

I don't know how long I read, but I fell asleep. I was out until almost sunup. I made some coffee and got a biscuit to eat from my saddlebags. I quickly devoured what I had and drank three cups of coffee. I saddled Dobbs and rode off toward the fort.

It wasn't long until I had the fort in sight. When I got closer to the fort I saw a lot of activity. I didn't know what it all meant. There may have been some sort of Indian uprising. When I was at the gate of the fort, I asked a corporal there to direct me to the officer in charge. He pointed to a building just across the yard. I rode over and tied Dobbs to the rail. I heard a voice inside say to enter after I knocked on the headquarters' door. I opened the door and entered, and then I introduced myself.

"Howdy, I'm Wil Gannon. I hope I'm not interrupting something important."

"Not at all, Mr. Gannon. I am Colonel Brumann. We were just discussing the Indian situation. It seems about a week ago, Colonel George Armstrong Custer and the whole 7th U.S. Cavalry were killed in the northern plains at Little Big Horn. We have been instructed to keep a watch on the Indians in our area. I think that they are making plans in Washington to do something big. We just don't have word of their plans as of yet."

"That explains the activity I've seen here. I have also seen the Kiowa and the Apache out of their normal routine. I am here to see if y'all have seen or heard of two men coming from Texas. One is William A. Hudman, and the other man is John Wild Horse. William or Bill is a large burly man, and John Wild Horse is a half Indian man. They ride a black stallion and a paint horse. These two men killed and robbed my good friend in Dodge

City, Kansas. I am on their trail. They were said to be in the New Mexico area."

"Mr. Gannon, I haven't seen these men, but I think some of the people on the Santa Fe Trail rode in and reported being robbed by men that fit that description. It appears that they are headed for Santa Fe."

"Thanks, Colonel. I will be on my way. Maybe I can catch up with them at Santa Fe."

"Good luck, Mr. Gannon."

I left the post and went to the mercantile. I picked up some supplies that I needed then headed for Santa Fe. I passed several groups of wagons that were also on their way to Santa Fe. When darkness set in, I grew weary of the trail, and Dobbs showed signs of being worn out. I saw a camp just ahead. I decided to stop in and see if they minded sharing their fire. The air near some of these mountains after dark was getting really cold. I thought maybe after another day or so I would be at Santa Fe. I came up to the camp and announced that I was coming in.

"Howdy, folks. Mind if I come in and share your fire?"

"Sure, cowboy. Come on in."

"Howdy. I'm Wil Gannon."

"We are the Southerich family. We came to start a new life here in the West."

"I bet you didn't think it was going to be as hard a trip as it is. The farther west you go, the harder it is to travel."

They had just fixed something for their supper that smelled good.

"Mr. Gannon, would you like to join us? There's plenty."

"Well, if you don't mind, and there's plenty, don't mind if I do."

They handed over a plate, then Mr. Southerich began to offer a prayer for the food. I guess I had seen this, but I didn't practice it myself. Although, after reading some in that Bible, I could see the reason for prayer. I think a person had to believe in God. After the prayer, they began to eat and so did I. They were silent for a while, and then Mr. Southerich began to speak.

"Mr. Gannon, are you a believer?"

"Mr. Southerich, I really don't know if I can answer that just yet. I have some thought on it and have been reading this Bible that I found in my friend's things after he died. I guess I would have to say I just don't know a whole lot about the subject just yet."

"I asked, because, as a preacher, I like to see as many as I can become believers. We are on our way out to start a new church here in the West. What brings you here, Mr. Gannon?"

"I am on the way to find the men that killed my friend and bring them to justice. I have been looking for them for a long while now. I heard they were somewhere here in the New Mexico Territory."

"What do you plan to do when you find them?"

"I plan to take them back to Kansas, to Dodge City, I guess."

"I wish you a safe journey, Mr. Gannon. I know

it can be dangerous looking for killers, but it is also dangerous just going through the country."

"Thanks, Mr. Southerich. I know of the dangers, and I am willing to risk it to find them. Folks, I think it's going to be a long day tomorrow. I plan to make it to Santa Fe, so I think I am going to turn in for the night."

"Goodnight, Mr. Gannon."

I lie there by the fire and thought about those folks and why they had come out here. I thought about finding those men. I found myself thinking about that lady back in Lost Creek.

CHAPTER FIFTEEN

I woke up early. The sun wouldn't be up for some time. The sun was always longer coming up in the mountainous areas. Getting Dobbs saddled in the dark and keeping quiet was not so easy, but it didn't take long. I didn't want to wake the others there at camp.

I knew the sun would be up soon and I would be able to see the mountains to the north. I enjoy the mountains. The desert-like area I had been through is pretty in its own way, but not like the mountains. The stars seemed to be larger there in the high country. They seemed to be close enough one could reach out and touch them. The air was giving off a pine scent from the trees.

The Pecos River was just ahead. I hadn't been west of the Pecos in a while. With it becoming light, everything looked green and fresh. On rocky ground, I hoped Dobbs didn't have any trouble with it. I would hate to have him go lame on me. I needed him as badly as he needed me. Dobbs probably could have gotten along without me. Having crossed the Pecos River, it wouldn't be long until I was at Santa Fe.

I traveled through the day and enjoyed the countryside. I wanted to make it to Santa Fe even though it was getting dark. I was beginning to see some light from some houses or cantina. When I got closer, I saw there were several cantinas on that side of town. I thought if I were going to find those two men I would have to look for them in a cantina or some place where they could find something to drink. When I reached the first cantina, I went in and looked for them. I could smell some fresh coffee so I ordered a cup and asked if anyone had seen the men I was looking for. My guess was that not everyone there could understand English. One of the Mexican men over at the end of the bar spoke up and said he had seen one of the men that I had described up the street at one of the other cantinas. I finished my coffee and headed to the cantina that he had told me about. That one was a little different than the one that I had just been. It was somewhat larger and seemed to have a little more class. I tied Dobbs to the post in front and heard laughing and talking going on inside. I heard my spurs jingle as I walked on the wooden boardwalk. They seemed to be louder at times, although I didn't know why. The doors were open, and I could see some men at the bar. Some men were playing cards at a table on one side. In the back corner, there was someone sitting at a table, but I could not see him well enough to tell who it was. The place was not very well lit. As I walked in I surveyed the rest of the room. My attention went back to the bar where there was a man standing.

From behind, he looked like the half-Indian man for whom I was searching. He was a lot taller than I had thought he might be. I would say between five and six feet tall. His hair was long and tied in the back with a strip of leather.

"John Wild Horse?"

"Yep, who's asking?"

"I'm Wil Gannon. I'm here to take you back to Kansas."

I had my hand on my gun just in case. He began to turn around. Halfway into his turn, he revealed a gun in his right hand. He was making his move. I tried to draw and fire at him but it was too late. He fired a shot, and I was sent whirling to the left and down to the floor. His shot hit me in the shoulder. I heard another shot just after the first, but I couldn't tell where it came from. I looked and saw John Wild Horse falling to the floor. He had a single gunshot in the forehead between the eyes. My attention went to the table where some men were playing cards. Smoke still lingered above the table. The man on the side near the wall was gathering his things and stood.

"Well, gents, that is enough excitement for me today. I think I will turn in."

He then went out the door as though nothing had happened. I was beginning to get up when someone on the other side came up.

"Here, let me give you a hand, Wil."

I turned and looked. It was Chris Toddle.

"Chris, what are you doing here?"

"I have been on the trail of those guys ever since

Kansas. This one is here alone. I hear the other one left here to head for gold and silver country up north. I am not sure where exactly. I thought this one might lead me to the other one. That is why I was just sitting in the corner over there waiting."

"I seen someone in the corner on my way in but I couldn't tell who it was. I then saw John Wild Horse at the bar. Who was the man that shot John?"

"I don't know for sure. I played a hand of cards with him, but I lost, so I got out. He is lightning fast with that gun. His gun was out, and fired, and back in his holster before I knew what was going on. I would like to say the way he plays cards, and as fast as he is with a gun, it was Doc Holiday. I don't know what he would be doing here."

"Yeah, Chris. I thought he was in Kansas."

"Well, no matter who it was, he saved your life. Let's see about your shoulder. Looks like the bullet went clean though. That's good. I think there is a doctor down the street. I'll get you to him and then we'll get you in a hotel room."

I went over to John Wild Horse's body to look for some of the money he had stolen. He had some, so I gave the bartender part of it to take care of his burial, and I put the rest in my pocket.

"Ok, Chris. I'm ready."

We headed up the street to a little place that didn't look like a doctor's office. It looked like a house or something. The man inside fixed me up. Chris and I headed for the hotel. It was a small place, but the room inside was neat and clean. When I stretched out on the bed, it didn't take long before I was out.

I must have been asleep off and on for several days. I really didn't know how long. When I sat up and looked around the room, there was not much in there. There was a small table, a chair, a lamp, a washbasin with pitcher, and a bed. I thought about John Wild Horse and the man who had shot him. Everything happened so fast. I don't think it lasted over a minute, if that long. I don't think I ever got my gun out of the holster.

"Oh, God. I don't know why I made such a promise." Tears began to well up in my eyes and stream down my cheeks. "God, it feels like it has been a lifetime since I have been in Texas. I sure didn't think that it would take this long to find these men. Talking to you seems odd. I just barely know anything about you, but I just have to talk. I don't have the kind of skills with a gun that a person needs to go after people like this. I almost got killed because I am slow with my gun. I don't really want to kill anyone. I just want to take them to stand trial for what they did. God, if you will help me find the other killer to fulfill my promises, I'll go back to Texas, become a farmer, and settle down."

Just then, Chris came in. I had forgotten that he was there.

"Who were you just talking to, Wil? There's not anyone in the room."

"I guess I was just talking to myself, Chris. I've been doing that a lot lately."

"Is that a sign that you are getting old?"

"Hey, watch it. I'm not that much older than you. How long have I been here?"

"You have been here a little over a week, Wil. You had a fever. You were in and out of it. I stayed by your bedside for most of the time, except when I went and rested. A Mexican senorita looked after you then. You mumbled in your sleep most of the time. I couldn't make out what you were saying. I heard you say "Jake" one time, and "Claudia" on another occasion. Who is Claudia?"

"That is just a lady I met back in Lost Creek before we made the drive to Dodge."

"Does she mean anything to you?"

"No, not so much yet. I would like to start courting her, though. She thinks that being a cowboy is not an honorable profession."

"Well, she is probably right. Most cowboys are a rough and rowdy bunch. They drink too much and get into fights. Some of them even like to mess with floozies."

"That's not like me, Chris. I have been in some fights, but not anything that I have started for fun or from drinking. I was in the wrong place at the wrong time and it happened."

"I would say she just knows what she has heard and seen from the ones that have been in town."

"I guess so, but I have to make her believe that I am not one of them. Meanwhile I need to finish what I started. Since it is late in the day, I will get an early start in the morning to find the other thief."

"I'll go with you to find the last of the two

thieves. You might be able to use my help, judging from the speed you tried to draw your gun in the cantina the other day. I am faster than you."

"I take it you are not as fast as the man that shot John Wild Horse."

"No. There are very few that are as fast as that. Some of them are on the wrong side of the law. We don't know how fast this Coonskin Bill is. I know if he is very fast, you won't be able to take him if he tries to go for it. Just let me go with you and I will have your back."

"That is what Jake used to say. Jake would say, 'I have your back.' I don't know, Chris. I will sleep on it and let you know in the morning."

"Fair enough. I will see you in the morning. By the way, I got you a new shirt. The one you were wearing not only had holes in it, but is also covered in blood."

"Thanks, Chris. My saddlebags are over there. Get what the shirt cost."

"I got it covered, Wil. I don't need any money. Call it a gift from me."

"Well, ok, Chris. If that is what you want."

"I'll get out of here and let you rest. I'll see you in the morning."

"Yeah, I'll see you in the morning, Chris."

I couldn't believe that I had been there so long. I would really have a hard time finding Coonskin Bill. If he were headed north into the mountains for gold, it would have been slow going because there was a lot of rough country there.

I guess it didn't take long to fall asleep. I woke up an hour or so before daylight. When I got dressed

I thought about Chris. I didn't want to get him more involved than he already was. I figured it would be better for me to go alone, so I gathered my things and left without him. When I left, I passed several missions or chapels on my way out of town. I thought about the people that used them to worship God. I found a trail that led out north of town.

When it became daylight, I could see mountains to the north and east. To the west of me was some sort of spires. They were red and strangely shaped. Some were tall and some were just barely rolling, little hills. I knew there were some Indians in the area that I would be going through, but I had no choice. I didn't want to go the long way around them. Some would be friendly tribes like the Navajo and Pueblos, but some would be Apache, a more warring tribe. I thought about them as I moved farther north. I constantly kept an eye out for any sign of Indians. I saw some smoke in some of the valleys to both the east and to the west.

It was getting late in the day and I saw some sort of village just ahead. I had been following a river for some time. I think it was the Rio Grande. When I reached the village there was another river that had joined the Rio Grande. The people in the village were watching me as I came into the area. They were Pueblo. A trading company was just ahead. Maybe there was a place I could stay for the night. I tied Dobbs to the post just outside and headed in to check things out.

"Howdy. Is there a place here I can stay the night?"

"Yes, I have a room. It's small, but I think you

should be comfortable. You can get something to eat here if you like."

"That would be good. I haven't had much to eat all day."

"Have a seat and I will get you something."

"Thanks, mister."

He brought out more food than I could possibly eat.

"Is there a place I can put my horse up for the night?"

"I can take care of him for you. Let me take you to your room."

"Thanks, mister."

He was right about the room being small. The bed sure looked inviting, though. I put my things down and just passed out on the bed. I woke up early again. The trader was already up and around. I smelled the coffee.

"How about a cup of that coffee?"

"Sure, mister. Would you like anything to eat?"

"Maybe a little something. I am in a hurry to get up to the gold country."

He returned with the coffee and food a short time later.

"I will have your horse ready for you as soon as you are ready to leave."

"Thanks."

"If you are going to gold country you should take Rio Chama River, the west fork of the river. They say there is a place along the way that is haunted. They say there are ghosts. It is some sort of Indian legend

I think. I have not heard of anyone being bothered by anything there, so I think you will be ok. When you get to Chama you should head north and west to get to the gold and silver country. You will pass Red Rock Canyon."

"Thanks, mister. I'll do that. I am not very familiar with these parts."

"Have a safe journey and God be with you."

CHAPTER SIXTEEN

I found Dobbs tied in front of the trading post as I went out to leave. He looked at me and shook his head as if he were ready.

"Ok, boy. We are ready to move on."

Dobbs and I headed out and stayed along the river. I was watchful for Indians. It seemed like it took forever to get anywhere. In the west at some distance, there had been some smoke. I didn't know if there were Indians or some settlement somewhere. Pine trees covered the area and the air was cooler. It had been quiet and uneventful so far. I didn't mind it being that way. Dobbs and I continued to follow the river.

The sun had started going down on the other side of the mountains. The air was a lot cooler than it had been just a short time before. I found a spot and made camp for the night. I tied Dobbs and took the saddle off. I gathered wood and built a fire. I thought some coffee would taste good. The smoke rose above the trees and the wood popped as it burned. The smell of pine wood burning was a lot different than the smell of the mesquite back in Texas. The smell of the coffee also filled the air. When the coffee was ready, I got some and ate some dried beef and a biscuit from the saddle-bags. I took Jake's Bible out and began to read by the glow of the fire. With the warmth of the fire and the coffee inside me, I got heavy eyed.

I guess I fell asleep reading the Bible. I awoke cold. The fire had almost gone out. I stoked up the fire and heated the coffee that was left from the night before. I placed Jake's Bible back in my saddlebags. Dobbs began to get restless from my stirring around. I spoke to him and assured him it was ok. He looked at me and nodded as though he understood. I finished the coffee and doused the fire with water from the river.

The sun would come up over the mountains soon even though it was early. The fragrance of pine was stronger in the morning air. I saddled Dobbs and we started out, once again following the river. When the sun began to come up over the mountain, there was an eerie fog set in along the river. Strange noises came from the woods. They seemed to have repeated them-selves each time, an echo or something in the mountain. Dobbs was really jumpy. I patted him on the neck.

"It's ok, boy. Calm down."

He continued to whinny and his eyes were wide. That went on for most of the morning. I continued to calm him as best I could. All at once we were out of the fog, and Dobbs calmed right down and acted as though there wasn't anything wrong. I was a little nervous myself through all that.

We hadn't made very good time. The fog and the rocks didn't help. They were hard for Dobbs to walk on. I decided to move out from the river a little ways to keep off some of the rocks. Maybe we would make a little better time.

My thoughts began to go back to Texas and the young lady that I had met in Lost Creek. I thought about what she had said to me. I also thought about some of the things I had read in Jake's Bible. Then I began to think about the killing back in Dodge and what had sent me on my journey. It was the middle of the summer. It had been several months since I left Lost Creek. I had hoped that I would be back there sooner. It didn't look as though I would be back there any time soon.

I continued in the direction I was going until it was dark. I decided to stop for the night. It got so dark amongst the thick forest and there wasn't any light from the moon. I just could not see to go on. I found a small clearing just ahead. I made coffee and read for a while, before stoking up the fire for the night. I looked over at Dobbs, he seemed to be doing fine. He had been watching me for some time, but at that moment he was looking away.

I stretched out and wondered what it would be like in the gold and silver country. Were there lots of people who had looked for gold or just a few scattered here and there? I wondered if there were any who had gotten rich. I didn't know where that thought had come from. I knew I wouldn't be rich. It would be an accident if that happened. I just wanted to be comfortable and worry-free.

Dobbs woke me the next morning after daylight. I guess he thought something might have happened to me.

"Settle down, boy. It's ok. I just slept in."

I saddled up, without any coffee or food, and I headed out. I rode all day, only stopping to give Dobbs water and to rest for a few minutes. By sundown, I thought I should have been close to Chama, it being along this route. I saw miners panning for gold along the river.

I found a good place to stop for the night by the river. I didn't know how far it was to Chama. I got Dobbs ready for the night and started some coffee. I began to dig in my saddlebags for something to eat. I hadn't eaten anything all day. I felt like I was about to cave in. I ate quickly and devoured several cups of coffee. I checked on Dobbs and turned in for the night.

I was awakened early by something that I heard near the river. I sat up and listened to try to figure out what had awakened me. I didn't hear anything. I looked at Dobbs, but he didn't act like anything was going on. I passed it off as something I may have dreamed. After making some coffee, I gathered up my things and headed out once again. I rode about an hour, and there I was in the middle of Chama. I didn't realize I was that close.

Chama was a small mining community, and it looked like they had started doing some logging. There was a sawmill to the east of the main part of town, a small mercantile and trading company, a hotel, a blacksmith and livery, a saloon, and a few houses. The other end of town looked like they had started a tent city. I worked my way through the people who filled the street. I finally made my way to the saloon. I knew Coonskin Bill would be in a place like that. I didn't think he would be the kind to go out and work trying to find gold. He would more than likely wait to find someone that had made a strike and rob him. I tied Dobbs to the post in front of the saloon and started in. The saloon faced the east and the sun was shinning in through the door. The saloon doubled for a diner. They had coffee going inside and people were eating. When I had finally reached the door, I stood there looking in and all around the room. People in the room stopped what they were doing and looked at the door. They could not tell who I was because the sun at my back kept my face shadowed. I continued over and sat at an empty table. As I came in, most of the people went back to what they were doing. Some were still curious and watched as the man from the bar came over with some coffee.

"Howdy, mister. Coffee and something to eat?"

"Sure, I haven't had a hot meal in a while."

He sat the coffee down and headed to get me what they were serving. When he returned, I decided to ask him about Bill.

"Has there been a man here that goes by Coonskin Bill or William Hudman? He is a large burly person. He rides a black stallion."

"I don't know if the man you ask about is the one a miner talked about or not. He sounds like the one. A miner came in here a few weeks back and said a man with similar description had robbed him. He said he thought someone had called him Bill. They said he left out of town and went to the north and west."

"It's likely he's the one I'm looking for. Thanks."

I paid him for the meal and made my way out the door to leave. I didn't make it to Dobbs before a miner came up to me.

"Mister, I couldn't help overhearing you ask about that man in there. I saw that man about two weeks ago. He was talking to another man and told him he was going to a place richer in gold and silver up north, a place west and then north through a pass, in Colorado I think. I heard that they are making Colorado a state this year some time. By the way, why are you looking for this man?"

"He and his partner killed a friend of mine back in Kansas. His friend is dead now. I am going to take this man back to Kansas."

"Did you kill his partner?"

"No, I really don't know who the person was that killed him. He looked a lot like Doc Holiday, but I'm not sure. He didn't stick around for us to ask questions."

"Well mister, I hope you find this man. Good luck."

"Thanks. I just hope it don't take forever to find him."

CHAPTER SEVENTEEN

I mounted Dobbs and headed out on the trail that led northwest. Since it was still early in the day, I thought maybe I could put a few miles behind me before dark. The going would be a little tougher.

After three days I was at the base of the pass. The mining camp would take a lot longer than that to get to. I stopped and rested since it was late in the day. I camped near the river thinking that I would get an early start. I tied Dobbs in a grassy spot for him to graze. I put my saddle and gear in an area just a little way over. Knowing it would get cold after dark, I gathered wood and started a fire. I decided to make coffee and read some from Jake's Bible. After reading a while, I came to a line. I stopped and thought as I read it again.

"I will call upon the Lord, who is worthy to be praised: so shall I be saved from mine enemies."

My thoughts took me away for a while, then I was back to reading. I continued to read until after dark. I stoked up the fire and decided to try to sleep. I heard the crackle of the fire, creatures in the woods, and the river as it ran over the rocks going downstream.

I guess it was the sound of water I heard just before I went to sleep because when I woke up early the next morning that was on my mind. The sound of the river was not as loud as it was the evening before. I didn't know why.

I gathered my things and saddled Dobbs. I took him over to the river for some water. I stood there waiting for him to get his drink and noticed that the river was not running as full as it was the evening before. When he finished we headed north once again. I noticed that Dobbs was not walking as well as he should. I looked down at his hooves. They were pretty rough. I had to move a little slower for Dobbs. I thought maybe there would be a place to get him tended to at that mining camp.

Dobbs and I followed the river for about a day and a half on the rocky ground. It was pretty slow going for Dobbs. I climbed down and walked with him for a long way, on and off, to give Dobbs a break. We left the river after the first day and began to climb up the pass. About noon on the second day in the pass, Dobbs began to limp with his front left hoof. I began to walk all the time with him. It was really slow going. I reflected on the things I had been through and what I might expect when I got to the mining camp, if William Hudman was there. I didn't know what I was going to do if he wasn't. I didn't know where to go then. I guess I would have figured it out when the time came. Meanwhile, it was getting dark and the temperature was really dropping. I saw a good place for us to stop and camp for the night. Maybe Dobbs would be better the next morning after some rest. I took the saddle off and got Dobbs comfortable for the night. I gathered some wood for a fire and made some coffee. I found a little something to eat in my saddlebags to go with the coffee. Dobbs was pawing at the ground some with that bad foot and letting out an occasional whinny.

"It's ok, boy. You'll be ok. I'm going to have someone take a look at your foot when we get to the mining camp."

He went up and down with his head in approval as if he knew what I had said. I unrolled my bedroll after I had eaten and lay with my head on the saddle. I was worn out. I must have fallen asleep very quickly. I didn't remember anything after that. I woke up feeling cold. The fire had died down and was almost out. I stoked it up and made some coffee to warm up again. It looked to be a few hours before daylight. I knew Dobbs would have needed more rest, so I stretched out again, only to fall asleep soon after. The next time I woke up, the sun was up and the fire was totally out. I got up and checked on Dobbs. He seemed to be a little better. I gathered my gear and we walked on up the pass. It was the middle of the afternoon when I saw some smoke in a little valley coming from some houses. It took us the rest of the afternoon to get down into that valley. There were mountains all around, one dusty street, and a river that ran on one side of the camp. I looked for a blacksmith or livery for Dobbs. I found one at the other end of the camp.

"Howdy. I have a horse that has a limp. Can you take a look at him and see what you can do?"

"Sure, mister. Which foot is giving him trouble?"

"His left front foot."

He quickly took a look and put the foot down.

"I think it is stone bruised. He needs to be trimmed, and he needs new shoes. I can take care of all that, but he is going to have to rest that foot for a few days."

"That'll be fine. I am going to be here for a few days anyway. Is there a place I can stay, clean up, and get something to eat?"

"Sure mister, just over there at that saloon."

I looked at where the man was pointing.

"Thanks."

I turned and headed for the saloon. It looked like a nice place. I was a little surprised to see something like that in a little mining town. I stepped onto the wooden boardwalk in front and walked to the door. I surveyed the room and the people inside, then went in. I walked across the room to the bar.

"Howdy. I need to get a room and a bath."

"Bath back there and room upstairs."

He handed me a key and I headed for the bath. It was a little room in the back where they had an odd shaped tub and a stove to heat the room and the water. A lady, somewhat older than me, came in from another room.

"Hi, I'm Be'Anne. You looking to get a bath?"

"Yes, ma'am."

"You can remove your clothes in there and I will get your water ready."

"Yes, ma'am."

I went to an area on the other side of the room that had a portion curtained off. I waited there until she had it ready and left. I had almost forgotten what a hot bath felt like. It sure felt good on my tired bones. I lay in the water until it was almost cold. After I dressed, I gathered my gear and headed for my room. Four rooms were upstairs. My key had a number that corresponded with the number on a door in the front end of the hall. I went in, put my gear down, and looked out the window onto the street. The sun was just about down and it was almost too dark to see anything. I looked at the bed and then I felt my stomach growl. My stomach had done that a lot. I headed back down to get something to eat. I found a little table in the back corner of the room. The lady that had drawn my bath came over.

"I would like whatever you have to eat. I am about to starve to death, I think."

"I have some goat stew left and some coffee."

"That will be fine, ma'am."

I watched as some miners came in. They started drinking and talking about what they had dug up. For some of them, it was probably all bragging and nothing to show. One miner at the end of the bar not only told about his, but he pulled out a big gold nugget and showed it around. As big as it was, I didn't think that was a very good idea. Someone would want to steal it from him. Just then, the lady returned.

"Thanks, ma'am."

She brought a large plate of stew. I had it eaten in no time at all. The miners continued to talk and get louder. I finished my coffee and headed for my room. I put my hat and gun on the table by the door and headed for the bed. I sat down and pulled my boots off. I laid back, stretched out, and fell fast asleep. I woke up the next morning with the sun shining in the window. I couldn't believe I had slept so long.

CHAPTER EIGHTEEN

The sun was well over the mountains, although it was morning, it was very late for me. I put my boots on, grabbed my hat and gun and headed downstairs. From the top of the stairs I saw that all the miners were gone. There were only a few people eating. I walked over to the bar and asked for a cup of coffee. In front of me were two large mirrors. I could see two paintings of women on the other wall in the mirror and a piano at one end of the wall by the door. I began to drink my coffee when a man walked in the door. All I saw was a large silhouette of the man in the mirror. The sun was at his back so I couldn't see his face. He paused as he came in. I had my hand near my gun because I didn't know what he was going to do. He walked over to the other end of the bar and ordered a whiskey. I kept my hand at my gun as I watched him in the mirror. The miner I saw the night before came in with his gun drawn and screaming.

"Give it back or you're a dead man."

The big man turned to face him.

"What are you talking about?"

"The gold. You took it. Give it back."

The big man started to go for his gun when the miner shot three times. The room filled with gun smoke. The smell of gunpowder was strong in the room. He must have hit him in the heart, lungs, and in the stomach judging from where the blood was coming from. He was dead almost instantly. The miner walked over, dug in his pockets, and pulled out the gold I had seen the night before. I walked over and looked at the man dead on the floor. I thought it might have been William Hudman. I looked at the miner.

"Is this man William Hudman, Coonskin Bill?"

The miner was quick to answer.

"Yep, he said he was Bill Hudman."

He was over six feet tall and almost as broad as the doorway. His face was covered with a reddish brown beard with some gray. He wore a coonskin hat and a gun on both hips.

"This is the man I had been looking for all the way from Kansas. He killed my friend there in Dodge City. I was going to take him back to Kansas. I guess you saved me the trouble."

I knelt down and dug in his pockets. I retrieved what money I could find.

"Well, this is not all the money he stole, but it will have to do."

I handed the miner some money.

"Here is some money. Find the undertaker, tell him his name, and give him this for his burial."

"Ok, mister. If that is what you want."

"It is."

I went back over to finish my coffee. I stood there looking at the man that had killed Jake. I couldn't believe that it was over and I didn't have anything to do with it. It seemed that the man would have met his demise without me going after him. I guess it was the higher power I spoke to Jake about. God was what I'd been reading about in Jake's Bible. I guess He takes care of His own one way or another.

I threw back the last swallow of coffee and headed out to check on Dobbs. When I stepped out the door, I looked both ways and saw that everyone was going about their own business as if nothing had ever happened. As I walked across the wooden boardwalk, the sound of my spurs seemed to be so loud. I didn't remember hearing them in a while. Sounds and smells were so much clearer at times.

I cut across to the northeast to the blacksmith. I noticed that there was a name for the town on the front of one of the buildings across the street. Silverton Dry Goods was the name on the business down from the blacksmith. I looked around the mountains to find there were mines dotting the hills all around. My eyes went to the front of the blacksmith shop. The man I had left Dobbs with the day before was working on a wagon wheel. When I had gotten closer, I saw Dobbs in one of the stalls around to the side.

"Howdy. Is my horse better today?"

"Yes, mister. He's a lot better now that he has a

trim and new shoes. I think he still needs to rest that left front foot another day or so."

"I'm sorry. I never gave you my name. I'm Wil Gannon."

"I'm Rupert Tussel, but they call me Mouse. Good to know you. I heard shooting at the saloon. Was that you doing the shooting?"

"No, a miner had a dispute with a man over his gold, although, the man he shot is the man I came here looking for. He robbed and killed my friend back in Kansas."

"I guess your hunt is over."

"Yes, I think I will be heading back to Kansas soon. Do you think that my horse will be good enough to travel tomorrow?"

"I think he will be ok by then."

"Good, I will come and get him in the morning. I will pay you now for everything in case I leave out before you are up."

"Sure, five dollars should cover everything."

"Here's the five, and thanks Mouse."

"You're welcome, Wil. Have a safe journey back to Kansas."

"Thanks, I will. I hope all my troubles are behind me for now."

I headed for the undertaker's place up the street. When I walked in the door I saw that he had William Hudman just about ready to bury.

"Howdy, I'm Wil Gannon. Is William Hudman ready for his burial?"

"Well, this man is ready for his burial, but he is

not William Hudman. We buried him earlier this year. I don't know who this man is."

"He is the man that killed my friend and I followed him from Kansas. He called himself William Hudman, Coonskin Bill."

"He may have called himself that, but he is not William Hudman. William's family can tell you that."

"Just mark his grave 'killer' and 'thief' that got what God gave him."

"Ok, Mister Gannon. You are paying for it."

"Good day, sir."

I headed out and went to the Silverton Dry Goods. I figured I would stock up, since they probably wouldn't be open when I got up the next morning to leave. As I walked in, I looked around the room. I saw all kinds of mining tools, like picks and shovels, metal pans, and skins and blankets, along with the food they had.

"Howdy. Please give me some of that cured meat, some of the biscuit things, and a couple of pounds of coffee. I think I'll have one of those blankets and a jacket, too. And give me a jar of them pickled eggs and three cans of beans. I think that will be all I need for now."

"Ok, mister. Here you go. Where you headed?"

"I'm headed back to Kansas. I have some unfinished business there."

"Have a safe journey."

"Thanks."

I gathered what I had purchased and headed to my room. There was a man playing the piano. Some of the miners had gathered at the bar bragging about their find again. I went upstairs and loaded my saddlebags with the food. I laid the blanket and coat on the table. Knowing it was going to be my last time for a good meal in a while, I went downstairs and sat at the same table I had the previous night. The lady came up the way she had before.

"What do you have to eat today, ma'am?"

"We have steak and mountain greens."

"That sounds good, and I'll have some coffee with that, please."

I sat there again watching the miners, but the miner that had killed the man earlier, didn't show off anything that time. He just said he had a fair day but nothing to brag about.

The steak came. I looked at the mountain greens. They were different than anything that I had eaten before, so I tried them. When I had eaten every bite, I washed it down with several cups of coffee. I listened to the piano for a while then headed for my room. I wasn't looking forward to the long trip back, but I wasn't going to stay there any longer than I had to. The mountains and trees were pretty, but I had had enough of that place.

I woke up early the next morning. It was up about two hours before sunup. I gathered my things and headed for the blacksmith. The blacksmith had gotten up early, too. He was in the stall with Dobbs giving his foot a rub and had him saddled.

"I didn't expect to see you this early, Mouse."

"I often get up early to get some of the miners'

things finished before they go to their claims. I knew you were wanting to get an early start, so I came over here to get your horse ready."

"Thanks, Mouse."

"You just be careful and take care of this guy."

"I will. Thanks again."

I loaded my things on Dobbs. I walked him out of the livery and down the street. I decided I would walk Dobbs for a day or two to give his foot more rest. It took me a few days to get over the pass and back down again. I then headed southeast through New Mexico to Santa Fe. I figured once I was in Santa Fe it would be easier to go to Kansas on the Santa Fe Trail.

CHAPTER NINETEEN

I had finally gotten back in Dodge City, but it took me over three weeks to get there. I was just glad there were no problems along the way. I think Dobbs was back to himself. His foot didn't seem to be bothering him.

I stopped in front of the undertaker's. I wanted to add to the marker on Jake's grave. I found some paper and wrote what I wanted and handed it to the undertaker.

"I would like to add to Jacob Norton's marker. I would like to see it before I leave. Do you think you will be able to do it today?"

"Yes–Mister Gannon, is it?'

"Yes, thanks."

I turned and left. I headed for the Marshal's office. When I entered, there was someone else in the Marshal's office. It was the Assistant Marshal, Ed Masterson.

"Howdy, I'm Wil Gannon. I was here in Dodge

some time back, and my friend Jacob Norton got killed. I think you went out looking for the guys that did it, but were unsuccessful. Marshal Deger was here at the time."

"He is still Marshal. I am the Assistant Marshal Ed Masterson. I think I remember that. We went out, but didn't find them. It was like they just vanished in thin air."

"Well, I tracked them from here to Texas, then New Mexico, and finally to Colorado. The first of the two was killed in Santa Fe. The second was killed in Silverton, Colorado. Although I was there when they both were killed, I didn't kill ether one. I do feel good that it fell to someone else. My intentions were to bring them both back here to jail."

"Marshal Deger will be glad that someone took care of them."

"I just thought he might like to know. Have a good day, Mr. Masterson."

"A good day to you, sir."

I headed for the same hotel I stayed at after the drive. When I walked up to the desk, the clerk remembered me right away.

"Hello Mr. Gannon. Will you be needing a room?"

"Yes. I will only be here for the night, and then I'll be headed for Texas."

"I think this is the same room you were in the last time. Will it be ok?"

"That room will be fine."

I took Dobbs to the livery, gathered my things,

and headed back to the hotel. I looked into the dining room and decided to put my gear in the room so I could go back to eat something. They had good food the last time I was in. When I sat down to eat, a lady came over to the table.

"I bet you don't remember me, do you? I am Colonel Brown's wife. I met you briefly the last time you were here. Your friend had just been killed so it wasn't the best of circumstances."

"Yes, I remember you now. You are right. That was just after he had been killed. I don't think I was myself then."

"Understandable, I'm sure, Mr. Gannon."

"Have you had a chance to see your husband since then?"

"Yes, I have. He visited me here a few weeks back."

"I trust he is well."

"Yes, he is. I think you look like you feel better, Mr. Gannon."

"Yes, ma'am. I think I am feeling better. The matter of the killing has finally been put to rest."

"That's good, Mr. Gannon. Well, it's been nice talking to you again. Take care."

"Yes, ma'am. And you do the same."

I ordered a steak and some coffee. After I finished, I headed back to my room. When I lay down and closed my eyes, my head was flooded with the events from my last visit to Dodge. It was as though I had lived it all over again. I guess it went through my head until I was asleep. I woke the next morning with sun shining in the window. It was another one of those nights I slept past sun up, something I didn't do very often.

I gathered my things and headed for the livery. I put everything on my saddle and took Dobbs down the street to the cemetery. There was a hitching post outside. I tied Dobbs and went to the spot where Jake was buried. I looked down at the marker. The undertaker had made the change. It read:

JACOB NORTON
FRIEND TO ALL,
A GODLY MAN
KILLED BY TWO BAD MEN,
MAY YOU REST IN PEACE

I liked it. I knelt down and put my hand on his grave once more.

"Well, Jake. It is finished. Rest in peace and God be with you."

I stood up, turned and walked away, never to look back. My job there was done and I was going to Texas. I climbed in the saddle and pointed Dobbs south, the direction we came in with the cattle. The Army had taken care of many of the Indians, so I felt safer on the trip to Texas. I rode long days and only slept for a few hours at night. A few days into the Oklahoma Territory, I came upon Russ O'Bannon and his wife, Christal. They had built a new house since I was there during the drive.

"Howdy, Mr. O'Bannon. How are you and your wife doing?"

"We are doing just fine, Mr. Gannon. Where is your friend, Jacob Norton?"

"I buried him back in Kansas."

"I'm sorry to hear that, Mr. Gannon. Where are you headed now?"

"I am headed back to Lost Creek in Texas."

"Won't you stay the night and have supper with us?" asked Mr. O'Bannon.

"I have been in a big hurry to get back, but I think I can stay over and give Dobbs a little rest."

"Good, I'll tell Christal you are going to stay over."

I put Dobbs in the corral and headed for the house. They insisted that I sleep in the house instead of the barn. That evening at supper, the conversation was quiet. I just didn't have lot to say, and I think they knew why. They wanted to give me their bed, but I said that I would be comfortable on the floor. I woke up early the next morning and left quietly. I saddled Dobbs and was on my way.

I continued to ride long days and slept only a few hours at night. I was just glad that all those rivers we crossed in the spring were way down. Late that evening I saw the Silver Spur Ranch. It didn't look any different than when I had left. John must have heard me ride up. He was out on the porch when I reached the house.

"Howdy, John."

I got down off Dobbs, tied him to the post, and stepped onto the porch.

"How are you, Wil?"

"Just fine, John. I am sorry about everything.

Here is all the money I could get back. I know it's not as much as it should have been for the cattle, but I can work and make it up to you."

"No, you don't have to do that. I'll take only half of what you brought back. I want you to keep the rest for your work and trouble you went through. I'm sorry about Jake. I know how close you two had become over the years."

"Thanks, John. I am going to be quitting the ranch to find me a farm to buy. This money will be a good start for me. I know of some land west of here and I think I can get for a good price. I am going to gather the rest of my things and I will be gone first thing in the morning."

"You don't have to leave so soon, Wil."

"Yes, if I don't, I may never leave. Besides, I want to marry a young girl in Lost Creek. She won't marry or have anything to do with a cowboy."

"When did this come about, Wil?"

"Just before we left I met her, and while I was gone, I made my mind up."

"If that is what you have to do, Wil, I won't stand in your way. Good luck to you."

"Thanks, John."

I turned, got Dobbs, and headed for the bunkhouse. I could smell something cooking inside. I wondered if Cookie was still fixing the meals. Sure enough, he stepped out just as I tied Dobbs to the post in front.

"How you doing, Wil?" Cookie said caringly.

"Just fine, Cookie. Still making them beans and such?"

"Yep. Come on in. You are just in time for supper."

After we sat down for supper, Cookie and the others just sat there earnestly, looking at me like they were waiting for me to tell them something. Knowing what they wanted to hear, I started in.

"Well, I guess y'all want to hear about my journey. After I left Dodge I found the first one, John Wild Horse, in Santa Fe. A man I thought was Doc Holiday killed him with one shot in the forehead between the eyes. The other man, William Hudman, or whoever he was, died in Silverton, Colorado. A miner shot him right in the heart. I never drew my gun on either one of them."

"What do you plan on doing now, Wil?"

"I am going to buy a farm and marry that girl I met in Lost Creek, Cookie."

"She sure is a pretty thing. I hope that makes you happy."

"I think it will, Cookie. I'm leaving here first thing in the morning."

"Where is the place you think you might buy?"

"It's west of here about two days. Well, it's been good catching up with you boys, but I think I'm going to take care of Dobbs and turn in for the night."

I headed out, put Dobbs in the corral and gave him some feed. I took in my gear and crawled into my bunk. I could hear the boys talking about what I told them while some were playing cards.

I woke up early the next morning and gathered

all my things. I walked to the door as quietly as I could, but Cookie heard me anyway.

"That you, Wil?"

"Yep."

"I figured you would leave well before daylight. Here is something for you to eat on your trip."

"Thanks, Cookie."

"If you decide to marry that girl, I want to be at your wedding."

"Oh, you will, Cookie. Everyone is going to be there. I wouldn't have it any other way," I walked to the door, "until then."

"Yep, then."

CHAPTER TWENTY

I rode a day and a half to the owner of the farm I was going to buy. I made my deal with him and headed for the place to look it over. I was glad the farm had a house so I wouldn't have to build one. When I got to the farm, I found that it had not been worked for some time. I spent the night in the house and cleaned it a little.

The next morning I headed for Lost Creek. It was almost dark the second day when I arrived in Lost Creek. I looked up the street and there wasn't much activity. I looked a little farther and I saw the little white church at the end of the street. There was some light inside. I decided to ride there and visit with the preacher. I tied Dobbs to the post in front and walked to the door. I stood there for a long time feeling strange, and then I went in. The preacher was at the front, kneeling with his hands clasped. When he got up, I headed down the aisle until I was beside him.

"I'm glad you made it. I had a feeling that someone would be here about now."

"How did you know?"

"Just a feeling I get sometimes."

"I had a strange feeling just outside the door. Must be something similar."

"I suppose so."

"I was wondering something. If I wanted to be baptized, what would it take?"

"You would have to know God and would have to believe in Him."

"I do."

"Then I think you are ready."

"When can I do it?"

"We can do it tomorrow. It's Sunday and I have some others to baptize."

"That's great. I'll be here."

"See you in the morning then."

I turned and walked out feeling totally different for some reason. I took Dobbs to the livery and went to get a room at a boarding house down the street.

The next morning I got up just before the sun came up. I cleaned up and got dressed and waited until I saw everyone headed for the church. When I headed up the street to the church, I saw Claudia as she rode up to the church in a wagon. I froze. I hadn't planned on that. Then I thought, she would get to see a changed person and would be interested in seeing me. I continued until I was inside. I sat on the last bench in the back. The preacher talked about God then he said that some had asked to be baptized. He said to go out to the stock pond out behind the church. He offered a prayer and we all headed out to the stock pond. He baptized about a half dozen people.

"We have one more."

He looked my way.

"Sir, I am ready for you now."

I looked around and then headed over toward the preacher in the pond. I stood beside him.

"I baptize you, my brother in Christ, in the name of the Father, the Son and the Holy Spirit. Amen."

He then dipped me in the pond and raised me out. I didn't feel any different than I had last night in the church, although I knew I was different. While walking back to the church, I saw Claudia and headed over her way. When I caught up to her she looked at me like she had seen a new person.

"Miss Claudia, I don't know if you remember me or not, but I am Wil Gannon and I would like to marry you. I have thought about you ever since I met you."

"Mr. Gannon, I can clearly see you have changed, but I don't see cowboys."

"Miss Claudia, I am no longer a cowboy. I bought a farm about two days west of here and I want you to share it with me."

She stopped short and thought. She turned and looked at me.

"Yes, I will marry you, but you have to ask my father for my hand."

"I'll do that! I'll do that right now."

I turned and went to her father who was near the wagon.

"Mr. Bradley, I would like your daughter's hand in marriage. I ask your permission for that, sir."

"Have you talked to her?"

"Yes, sir."

"Then if she is in agreement, I give you my blessing."

"Thank you, Mr. Bradley."

I turned and went over to Claudia.

"He said he would give his blessing if you were in agreement with it. You still do, I guess."

"Yes."

"I would like us to be married here next Saturday. Is that ok with you?"

"If my family says it will be ok, then I guess it is fine with me."

"Ok. I will meet you here next Saturday, if I don't hear anything first."

"Ok."

I could hardly wait until Saturday. I got a new shirt and went to the Silver Spur Ranch to tell everyone. I stayed at the ranch until Friday evening, then I went to town for the night.

I thought about everything. I thought about how our life would be on the farm. I could hardly fall asleep but finally did. I woke up just as the sun was coming up. The birds were singing, the air smelled fresh, and the sky was clear. One couldn't ask for a more perfect day. The preacher said that I should be there about ten. It was just a few more hours until we were to be married.

I went down for breakfast. I ate so much I was stuffed. I continued to drink coffee and think about how beautiful Claudia was. She had long brown hair, blue eyes, and her face was so beautiful. I thought about how it would have been nice to have Jake there to share that time with me. I think he knew.

Time seemed to fly by. In no time at all, it was about a quarter til ten. I straightened my clothes and wiped the dust from my boots. As I was walking down the street to the church, I saw the boys from the ranch going to the church. They all met me at the door.

"Howdy, boys. Glad you could be here. Howdy, John."

"Wil, you sure look happy. I am glad for you."

"Thanks, John. I wish Jake could have been here."

"I think he is in spirit and in your heart."

"Yeah, he probably is."

I walked to the front of the church where the preacher was standing.

"I have something I have to tell you. My name is not Wil. That is a nickname they gave me because every time they wanted something done they said, will you do this, will you do that, so it stuck. My name is Lawny Dale Gannon. You should use it in the service."

"Ok, Wil. I mean Lawny."

A lady had begun to sing. I turned and looked at Claudia who was walking down the aisle with her father. She was so beautiful in her long white dress. She continued down the aisle until she was beside me. I took her hand and turned to the preacher.

"We are gathered here today to join this man and this woman in holy matrimony in the site of God and these witnesses. Do you, Lawny Dale Gannon, take Claudia to be your wife, to have and to hold from this day forward, for better or for worse, until death you shall part?"

"I do."

Claudia looked at me inquisitively. I think she was wondering about the name.

"Do you, Claudia, take Lawny to be your husband, to have and to hold from this day forward, for better or for worse, until death you shall part?"

"I do."

"For this cause shall a man leave his father and mother, and cleave to his wife; and they twain shall be one flesh, so then they are no more twain, but one flesh. What therefore God hath joined together, let not man put asunder. I pronounce you man and wife. You may kiss the bride."

I kissed her with my arms wrapped gently around her. I knew then that everything was right. We turned and faced the congregation and headed down the aisle for the door as husband and wife. They had a party for us at the schoolhouse next door. Everyone had a chance to visit.

We gathered our things and got on a wagon with Dobbs following. We headed west to our farm.

One of the boys yelled, "Hey, Cookie. You think he'll get better cooking with her than he had with you?"

Contact Ron Cannon
at canwriter@sbcglobal.net

or order more copies of this book at:

TATE PUBLISHING, LLC

127 East Trade Center Terrace
Mustang, Oklahoma 73064

(888) 361 - 9473

TATE PUBLISHING, LLC
www.tatepublishing.com